Ladies first . . .

Early that afternoon when their stagecoach jolted up the potholed streets of Gold Creek, the miners and store owners came rushing out to greet the Love Sisters. It was all that Longarm and Big Mamma could do to try and keep them from actually pulling the three frightened young women out of the coach and having a good time with them right in the street.

"Hold on!" Longarm shouted, setting the stagecoach's brake and jumping to his feet with his gun in his fist. "These are *ladies*."

"They're women," someone shouted. "And we sure need some new women in Gold Creek. So sit down and tell them gals to come out and show us their pretty faces."

Before Longarm could respond, Big Mamma stood up and levered a shell into her rifle. In a deep and menacing voice, she bellowed, "Anyone touches these ladies is gonna take a shortcut to the Promised Land!"

TABOR EVANS

LONGARM

AND THE LOVE SISTERS

JOVE BOOKS, NEW YORK

This is a work of fiction. Names, characters, places, and incidents are either the product of the author's imagination or are used fictitiously, and any resemblance to actual persons, living or dead, business establishments, events, or locales is entirely coincidental.

LONGARM AND THE LOVE SISTERS

A Jove Book / published by arrangement with
the author

PRINTING HISTORY
Jove edition / November 2000

The Penguin Putnam Inc. World Wide Web site address is
http://www.penguinputnam.com

ISBN: 0-515-12957-7

A JOVE BOOK®
Jove Books are published by The Berkley Publishing Group,
a division of Penguin Putnam Inc.,
375 Hudson Street, New York, New York 10014.
JOVE and the "J" design
are trademarks belonging to Penguin Putnam Inc.

PRINTED IN THE UNITED STATES OF AMERICA

10 9 8 7 6 5 4 3 2 1

Chapter 1

Deputy Marshal Custis Long wasn't accustomed to being called into work on one of his rare days off. He'd planned to spend the afternoon enjoying Denver's fine spring weather with Miss Lucy McCoy, a lovely young lady with laughing blue eyes and a bawdy sense of humor. But now, here he was, striding impatiently past the U.S. Mint at the corner of Colfax and Cherokee and then bounding up the stone stairs into the Federal Building. A messenger boy had been sent to tell him that there was a high-level and very urgent meeting he must attend and would he please wear his best suit and be at his most presentable.

"This better be important," Longarm muttered as he strode across the polished marble floor, boot heels echoing up and down the impressive hallway lined with oil portraits of forgotten former government officials.

"Hey, Custis!" Deputy Marshal Earl Weaver called, hurrying to overtake him. "Slow down!"

"I'm in a hurry," Longarm said. "I'd planned to spend this afternoon with a special lady and I'll be damned if I'm happy to waste it sitting in on some meeting."

"You might not have any choice."

"What," Longarm asked, coming to an abrupt halt, "is that supposed to mean?"

"Only that there's something big going on around here and I have a feeling you're about to get shafted again," Earl said. "The Director and Billy have people here all the way from Washington, D.C., and they look very important."

"Well, I'm *not* important, so whatever they have in mind shouldn't concern me one damned bit."

"You hope."

Longarm was in a hurry, but if he were walking into a terrible assignment, one that no one else would accept, he wanted to be prepared to instantly squash the request. He had spent enough years there to earn some seniority, but it was not past Billy Vail to conveniently forget that fact and send him off to some miserable place to do a thankless, nearly impossible job.

"Earl," he said, continuing down the hallway, "I don't care how far they came or how high up they are. I'll refuse whatever they offer. We've younger deputy marshals that hardly ever get out into the field. Why is it that veterans like you and me are asked to do all the dirty work?"

"Because we are the only ones that can handle the 'dirty work.'" Exasperation edged into the lawman's voice. "For example, I'm being sent to Montana tomorrow to try and settle a gawdamn range war that is brewing. And do you think that I'll get any support? Hell, no!"

"You got that assignment?"

"That's right. I was hoping you'd get it."

"Well, I wasn't," Longarm said, feeling relieved. "I heard about that trouble. Sheep men are finally banding together to fight the big cattlemen. I wouldn't want to step into that one."

"Amigo," Earl said, slapping Longarm on the back, "I'm not sure that what they have in mind for you upstairs might not be even worse."

"I can always refuse."

"And lose your job."

"Billy and the Director wouldn't fire me. They know I handle more than my share of the tough assignments."

"Just like I do. But in this case, I'm thinking that even our Director couldn't save your job if you refused these important officials."

"We'll see about that," Longarm said gruffly.

"Custis, don't go off on this half-cocked," Earl advised. "We need you in this department too much. Just remember that these Washington officials didn't come all the way out to Colorado just to have some lowly deputy tell them to go to hell."

"Where is everyone meeting?"

"Director's office." Earl winked. "You know Mr. Cardiff doesn't have a meeting in his office unless it is really important. Good luck!"

"Thanks," Longarm growled.

Feeling both irritable and defiant, he shoved one of his smelly nickel cheroots into his mouth as he strode toward the Director's office while brushing a strand of Lucy's blond hair off his vest. Because Longarm was both hated and feared by Denver's lawless element, he always wore his .44–40 Colt on his left hip, and meeting officials wasn't going to change that fact. Longarm favored the cross-draw, and just in case that was inconvenient, he had a nasty little hideout derringer attached to his watch chain so that it rested securely in his vest pocket.

Custis Long was a big man, and women considered him extraordinarily handsome with his handlebar mustache and wavy brown hair. And he was generally a tolerant fellow, but one who found government bureaucracy extremely galling and defined by endless conferences and meetings. Because he so loathed staff meetings, Longarm held faint hope that he would ever be promoted to marshal, but that was just fine as long as the pencil-and-paper-pushers left him alone.

3

Longarm came to a sudden halt before the Director's office with its large gold lettering on the door. He raised his hand to knock, but the door swung open and there he stood with his knuckles raised and a scowl on his ruggedly handsome mug.

"Come in! Come in!" Marshal Billy Vail and Director George Cardiff called, wide smiles creasing their scheming faces.

Longarm stepped into the Director's plush office for maybe the third or fourth time in all the years he'd worked out of the Denver Federal Building as a United States deputy marshal. In one corner of the huge room was a long mahogany table, and it was there that all the Washington, D.C., officials sat with their insipid grins.

"It is good to see you, Custis," the Director said, reaching up to slap Longarm on the back as if they were lifetime bosom buddies. "It certainly is a pleasure to see you on such a fine day."

Cut the crap, Longarm thought. What kind of miserable assignment have you got that would call for all this phony malarkey?

"Would you care for a *Cuban* cigar?" Director Cardiff offered, scenting the foul odor of Longarm's cheap cheroot. "I'm sure that you don't often have a chance to enjoy them."

"I would if I could afford the damned things," Longarm said brusquely.

The officials managed to laugh, but Billy Vail didn't look a bit amused by Longarm's brusque and tactless reply. "Custis," he said, "allow me to introduce the gentlemen in attendance. Starting with Congressmen Samuel Potts, whom I'm sure you have met a time or two."

"Not really," Longarm said, becoming increasingly anxious about the way he was being treated.

He shook hands with the Congressman, and then was

4

introduced to the Washington officials, who seemed tense underneath their exterior joviality.

"And finally," Billy said, "allow me the pleasure of introducing the United States General of the President's Office, Mr. Hamilton Page the Third."

Even Longarm, who cared nothing for politics, had heard of this man, who was said to be one of the most influential people in Washington and quite likely a future President of the United States. Slender and in his mid-fifties, Hamilton Page was elegant and stylish. There wasn't a hair on his head that was out of place and his manicured fingernails were coated with a clear, shiny polish. His perfectly tailored suit was black and a suitable contrast to his perfectly white teeth and starched shirt. To Longarm, Page looked more like an expensive mannequin than a human being.

"I'm delighted to meet you," the man of Washington said with an ever so slightly condescending smile. "Director Cardiff and Marshal Vail say marvelous things about your abilities. I gather that you are quite an extraordinary lawman. A really forceful fellow and man of the West."

Custis had never been comfortable with compliments, and this one made him downright nauseous. "I like my job, but it's small potatoes compared to yours."

"Nonsense," Page said modestly. "We are all doing what is best for our country, are we not?"

"When it pays well enough. Say, what is everyone staring at *me* for?"

The abruptness of Longarm's tone and question caught the high-ranking government official off guard. Hamilton Page recovered quickly, however, and said, "I like a man who doesn't beat around the bush. And you, Marshal Long, definitely fit into that category."

"Thanks, but it's *Deputy* Marshal, and you didn't answer my question."

"Marshal Long," Director Cardiff said, not bothering to hide his exasperation. "I think it would behoove you to be a little more pleasant."

"No, no! That's all right," Page said. "Deputy Marshal Long has asked a direct question and I will respond with a direct answer."

"That's appreciated," Longarm said, ignoring the dirty looks from his immediate boss and the Director.

"May I call you Custis?" Page asked.

"Sure."

"Well, Custis, we have a very important job, and both Mr. Vail and Mr. Cardiff have assured myself and my friends that you are indeed the very best man to handle this job."

"Which is?"

Page glanced at the men seated at the table, cleared his throat, and proceeded. "Are you aware that there have been a series of newspaper articles running in the East that have raised the awareness of people as to the plight of women living in Western mining towns?"

Longarm glanced at the blank faces of his boss and supervisor, then turned back to Page and said, "No, sir, I certainly have not. You see, I don't even read the local papers, let alone the Eastern ones."

"Of course not. You are obviously a man of action rather than an intellectual. Can you read?"

"I can," Longarm snapped, feeling insulted by the question.

"Well, then," Page said, "I'm sure that, after this meeting is over, you will find these . . . shall I call them exposés . . . of the suffering of women in mining towns to be of interest."

"Exactly what are you driving at?"

"The articles uncovered the plight of women in the mining camps, and that has raised quite a fervor of righteous indignation back East, especially among the more

6

privileged ladies. No one was aware of how hard, cruel, and unfair life is for women in mining camps."

"It's not too damned easy for the men either," Longarm bluntly reminded the official. "At least the women aren't being buried alive during mining cave-ins."

"No, I'm sure they are not. But according to these articles, women working in the mining camps labor under the most inhumane of conditions for extremely low wages."

"Most of the younger, prettier ones that work in the saloons and such make a ton of money."

Page's square jaw sagged, and Director Cardiff paled. Billy Vail recovered first and said, "Custis, you must admit that the ladies of the camps are quite often in dire straits. They get diseases, they get shot and stabbed, and they die young."

"Some of 'em do, some don't." Longarm took a moment to relight his cheroot. He puffed on it with satisfaction, then continued. "Billy, you remember Rose LaFancy. Why, she ended up marrying that mine owner and today is worth a fortune. And what about Bouncy Betsy? Remember how she used to . . . well, I heard she has a whole bunch of girls working for her and is rich as a queen. And what about—"

"Deputy Marshal Long," Director Cardiff interrupted with unconcealed exasperation. "I'm sure those are the exceptions. Most of the women who work in the camps suffer unspeakable poverty."

Longarm could see which way the wind was blowing. "All right. So what can anyone do about it?"

"That is a very good question," Page replied. "And I'll give you a very good answer. The newspaper articles caused such an outrage among thousands of readers that a charity was created specifically to assist mining camp women who deserve a helping hand."

"What charity?"

"They call themselves Love Sisters."

It was Longarm's turn to gape. "What!"

"A charity called Love Sisters has been founded and funded. The Love Sisters are coming out here in a few days to begin their important work helping the downtrodden women in the mining camps."

Hamilton Page smiled. "And the President himself has contributed a significant amount of money to this effort. You see, one of his very own granddaughters will be a Love Sister arriving in Denver."

Longarm groaned and took a seat.

"Her name is Miss Alice Fairchild. She is very proud and excited to be a Love Sister. Our President has specifically asked her to write to him directly as to the good work that Miss Fairchild and the other Love Sisters are doing in the mining camps this summer."

Longarm wanted to walk—no, run—out the door, but something told him that if he did so, his career as a law officer would suddenly end.

"Marshal Long," Page was saying, "are you beginning to understand the significance of this charity and the depth of commitment that the Love Sisters have for the exploited women of the West? Especially those enslaved amid the poverty, degradation, and squalor of the mining camps?"

"Yes, but why are you telling me this?"

Page turned to Longarm's Director. "Perhaps you should answer that question, George."

"Ordinarily," Director Cardiff began, "a mission such as this would be highly publicized. However, in this case, a decision has been made that these sisters . . . in order to avoid the limelight and the attraction of charlatans . . . will travel somewhat incognito."

"And how," Longarm demanded, "do they plan to do that?"

"They will present themselves as a troupe of entertainers. That way, they can really see what is going on and which women in the camps honestly need charitable assistance."

"Sir," Longarm replied, "that won't work."

"Why not!"

"The word will get out and their true identities and purpose will be known as fast as you can say 'scat.' And when that happens, the Love Sisters will be targeted by every charlatan and con artist within five hundred miles as being ready for picking. If these so-called Love Sisters have money to give away, I guarantee they will be robbed, cheated, and lied to until they don't know what or who to believe."

"Which is where you come in," Hamilton Page replied. "You are chosen to be not only their escort, but also their protector."

"Not a chance. In my opinion, which I know means nothing, the Love Sisters should remain back East," Longarm said flatly. "Otherwise, they will most certainly not be genteel ladies for long."

"That is exactly our concern!" Congressman Potts cried, rising to his feet and pounding the table. "Won't you please try to understand the difficulty of this situation and its importance!"

"I understand that a bunch of people back East became enraged by some newspaper writer who probably exaggerated things a fair amount to sell more copies. So then well-intentioned but naive upper-society women who have never been west of Boston have come forth to right a social injustice they do not understand."

"Is that your final word on this?" Hamilton Page angrily demanded.

Custis was also getting mad. How dare a bunch of foolish Eastern women get on their high horses and think that scattering some money around, and probably giving a bunch of hugs and shedding a few tears, was going to

9

make a real difference. Why, the mission was doomed before it began, and he'd bet that the Love Sisters wouldn't last two weeks in the wilderness before they raised their skirts and ran from the hills.

"Mr. Page, are you asking me if I *refuse* to participate in this ridiculous undertaking?"

"That's exactly what I'm asking."

"Then my answer is—"

"Custis," Billy Vail shouted, jumping between the two men, "come outside for a moment so that we might have a word in private."

"Billy, you can—"

But Longarm's boss cut him off by stomping hard on Longarm's toes and then dragging him out the door and slamming it shut behind them.

"Custis, are you crazy!"

"No. Are you?"

"This assignment will make or break not only your career, but also mine and that of our Director. Don't you understand that the *President of the United States of America* is watching what we do here?"

"Yeah, but this whole thing is ridiculous."

"I agree!"

Longarm blinked. "You do?"

"Of course," Billy said, leading Longarm a short ways down the hall where they could not possibly be overheard. "But do you really think that Mr. Cardiff or I had any choice but to go along with it? Our heads will be lopped off if it fails. That's why we both agreed that you—Deputy Marshal Custis Long—are the only man we have who has any chance of saving *all* our careers."

Longarm shook his head. "The Love Sisters are gonna be like chickens walking into the fox's den. And I'll tell you something else. A lot of the women will take them for easy marks just like the men will. How am I supposed to protect a bunch of society women who have no idea what kind of world they are stepping into?"

"I can't answer that," Billy replied. "And I'd go myself except that the Love Sisters are convinced that they should visit the mining camps under the pretext of being a working troupe of entertainers. Dammit, they will be shocked and probably fail, but their hearts are in the right place and we have to protect them!"

"At best they will be cheated and disappointed, fooled and laughed at," Longarm said. "At worst they'll be compromised and killed. Now I ask you . . . how will the President react if that happens?"

"It just can't happen," Billy said, looking desperate. "There will only be four or five of them and you'll pose as their wrangler."

"You mean I can't even say I'm a lawman?"

"That's right. If people saw you wearing a badge, the Love Sisters would never be able to pass themselves off as a traveling troupe of entertainers."

"Billy, the minute they hand out money, they will be exposed for what they really are. You know how fast news travels up in the mining camps."

"That's right. And I've told the Congressman and Mr. Page that the only way this could work is if the Love Sisters don't distribute money while they are touring. They'll have to take names and then send money later. That way, you won't have the added responsibility of carrying a lot of cash in their wagon."

"Billy, I just—"

"Custis, you can't refuse us. Remember, I have a wife and children. I've been your friend . . . haven't I?"

"Sure, but—"

"Didn't I even name you as the godfather of our first child?"

"Yeah, Billy, but—"

"And Director Cardiff is counting on us both. He has

said that if you are successful at this, you will receive a promotion to marshal."

"And get tied to a desk pushing papers like you? No, thanks."

"Then how about a month's leave with full pay?"

Longarm swallowed. "How long are the Love Sisters planning to tour?"

"Just a couple weeks. Maybe even less."

"But maybe more."

"Not a chance," Billy assured him. "You know that they'll hate those grubby mining camps, bad roads, and the cold, rainy weather. They will yearn for all the luxuries that they've long been accustomed to enjoying. Why, the tour might end in a week! However, you'd still receive your month paid vacation. And that's the Director's promise."

"This could be the worst mistake of my life."

"If you refuse, we will all be looking for jobs. Remember who hired you?"

"Yeah," Longarm said. "You did."

"A little help in return," Billy said quietly, "would be greatly appreciated. Just a couple weeks driving some high-society women around the gold and silver camps and playing wrangler and friend—that's all that Director Cardiff and I ask. And I've heard that Miss Fairchild is stunning."

Longarm scoffed at this bait. "You don't think I'm idiotic enough to get messed up with the *President*'s granddaughter, do you?"

"No . . . I guess not. And, to be honest, there is one other consideration that you ought to be aware of and it's one that can't be helped."

"Are you about to tell me that the assignment gets even worse?"

"No, better. You see, Custis, you wouldn't be the only

one protecting the Love Sisters. Apparently, their leader is quite . . . formidable."

He frowned. "Meaning?"

"Meaning that her name is Big Mamma and she stands well over six feet tall and is said to be tougher than nails but every inch a beautiful, capable woman. She's a crack shot and has been handpicked for her ability to defend and dissuade anyone from taking advantage of the President's granddaughter or the other Love Sisters."

Longarm grinned. "She might be the only one that I'll like."

"Then you'll do it?"

"All right, but in return, I want six weeks of paid vacation."

"Custis!"

"Six weeks and we've got a deal."

"Director Cardiff has no choice but to agree to that."

Longarm squared his shoulders. "Then let's get this settled in a hurry. I've got other plans for today and I'm not willing to waste any more time."

"Thanks, Custis."

"Six weeks. You tell him the minute we get inside his office."

"With all those officials around?"

"Find a way," Longarm said as he marched back into the Director's office. No one said a word until Longarm helped himself to a Cuban cigar, then said, "Love Sisters. It's a name that will attract attention. So when are they arriving in Denver so we can get this mission of mercy started?"

Hamilton Page was the first to pump Longarm's hand, followed by Director Cardiff, whose smile died when Longarm leaned close and whispered, "Six weeks, not four. Okay?"

"Uh . . . sure."

"Great."

13

After that, the meeting went just fine. Longarm discovered that the Love Sisters would be arriving in just three days, so there would be a lot of preparation work to do. Using that as his reason, he excused himself after a few minutes and headed off to see the lovely Miss Lucy McCoy.

Chapter 2

"What I still don't understand," Lucy McCoy asked as they left a nice cafe and started walking arm-in-arm through a city park beside Cherry Creek later that evening, "is why were *you* picked to protect the Love Sisters."

"I have no idea."

"Well, there must be some reason."

Longarm considered the question without much enthusiasm. After all, Lucy was a beautiful young woman and the night ahead held great promise. So far, he had not been able to get the lady into his bed, but he had a feeling that could happen, given exactly the right circumstances and timing.

"Maybe they think that I can get along with Big Mamma because I'm tall and so is she?"

"Oh, come on now! Surely you can do better than that."

"Well," Longarm said, drawing the woman into his arms and kissing her in the moonlight, "I don't mean to sound arrogant or overconfident, but I suppose they believe that these women will be safer under my watch than anyone else's."

Lucy giggled. "Why would they think that sending a wolf out to guard their lambs is a such a fine idea?"

"Because they know this wolf takes his job seriously." Longarm's right hand slipped from Lucy's waist to her lovely round bottom and he whispered into her ear, "I hope you aren't jealous because, once I'm responsible for the Love Sisters, I'm going to be a complete gentleman."

"Oh, sure!" she cried, laughing as she pushed his hand off her posterior. "I'm supposed to believe that!"

"My dear Miss Lucy, you don't know me quite as well as you might think," he said, trying to appear a tad offended. "I was raised in West Virginia, where ladies are both honored and respected."

"Custis, be honest for once. Do you respect me?"

"Of course!"

"Then keep your hands where they belong!"

Longarm's hopes were dashed. He could have enjoyed a romp in the bed with any number of more "worldly" Denver women, but Lucy McCoy was a tempting challenge. She was probably a virgin, though in her early twenties, and possessed a lot of spunk and spirit, qualities that Longarm found very attractive. But if this was how each of their evenings was going to end, he might be forced to seek other more willing women.

"Lucy," he said, "why don't we take a carriage ride out into the countryside this evening? It's not all that late yet and we don't have much time left to spend together before my assignment and . . ."

The lady was about to say no when she stiffened with fright.

Longarm turned to see what had alarmed Lucy, and found himself confronted by three rough-looking characters. There was enough moonlight to see that the largest of them clutched a six-gun in his grimy fist and the other pair held wicked-looking Bowie knives.

"Well, well," the largest of the trio said in a mocking voice with the gun in his hand waving slightly as he talked, "what do we have here? A pair of young lovers

16

about to enjoy a little humping down beside the creek?"

"Get lost," Longarm warned, easing a trembling Lucy around behind him so that she would be shielded from a bullet.

"What's the matter?" the leader asked, taking a step closer. "Mister, you aren't very friendly. Maybe we'd like some of that kissin' and lovin' from that pretty lady too."

"That's right," another agreed, licking his lips. "Why don't we *all* share in the fun? Hey, pretty girl, what do you think of that idea?"

"You boys are about to get arrested," Longarm said, starting to reach into his pocket to retrieve his badge.

"Hold it!" the man with the gun shouted, cocking back its hammer. "Keep your hands out in the open, mister."

"I'm a United States deputy marshal," Longarm told them as rage built up inside. "And all three of you are under arrest."

The shortest of the three giggled. "This fella must be the stupidest sonofabitch we ever robbed!"

"I am a federal lawman."

"Boys," the man with the gun said, "why don't you castrate this big fool while I take the young lady down to the river and show her what a *real* man can do."

"Custis," Lucy whispered, "this isn't going well!"

Longarm pushed her farther back behind himself and did a quick assessment of the situation. He was sure that these were professionals. The pair with Bowie knives held them cutting edge up, and looked as if they knew exactly how to castrate, then disembowel their prey. Just as ominous was the one with the pistol pointed at his chest, who had stepped to one side with a confident and malicious grin stamped across his hairy face.

"Tell you what," Longarm offered, desperately needing to catch them a bit off guard. "How about you fellas just take my gold watch and chain, all my money and jewelry, and leave us alone? Forget the arrest."

17

"My, oh, my," one of the knife-wielding duo said contemptuously, "I think the big marshal is finally getting scared!"

"Worried," Longarm corrected, "but not scared."

"Then you really are stupid," the man with the gun hissed.

"Look," Longarm said. "I am carrying an expensive gold watch and chain. Here, let me show it to you."

For just an instant, they forgot their murderous intentions, and that was enough time for Longarm's fingers to trace their way down the watch chain to his two-shot derringer. "Surprise, surprise," he told them as the nasty little derringer popped into view.

The three men reacted, but not fast enough. And although Longarm fired without bothering to take aim, they were close and his first bullet punched the pistol-packing man in the chest. The .44-caliber derringer spat flame and smoke a second time as Longarm pivoted and fired, striking the smaller of the knife fighters just below his protruding Adam's apple. The man collapsed to his knees, hands groping at his neck wound as blood gushed between his fingers.

The last and only surviving man stood frozen in shock.

Longarm balled his left hand and swung from down near his knees. His knuckles connected with the man's jaw, delivering a thundering uppercut. So great was the force of the perfectly timed blow that the man actually lifted off the ground. As he was coming down, Longarm grabbed him by the shirtfront and drove his knee upward into his groin, causing his victim to scream and drop his knife.

Longarm snatched the knife from the ground, then watched as the man with the bullet hole in his throat tried to breathe and speak at the same time.

"Oh, my gawd!" Lucy cried, staring at the dying man. "Custis, what . . ."

"Lucy, look away," Longarm ordered. "At this point, not even a surgeon could save his life."

Lucy walked a short distance off, sobbing. Longarm watched as the choking, gagging man reached up with both hands, beseeching him to do something to help.

"I wonder," Longarm said, watching the man's body begin to convulse in death, "how many couples you and your friends hurt or killed."

The man died horribly as Longarm went over to Lucy and said, "I'm sorry about this. I offered to give them a chance, but they were too stupid or greedy to accept. I'll need to take the surviving one to jail."

"What about the two you shot and killed?"

"We'll have to leave their bodies here. No one is likely to bother them other than maybe to rifle their pockets." Longarm reached out and took the young woman's hand. "Are you all right?"

"Not really. Look. More people."

Longarm turned to see an elderly foursome staring at him and the grisly sight of the dead. They had probably attended a local theater and were now walking home. Longarm beckoned them over and when they refused, he released Lucy's hand and hurried to their side.

"I'm Deputy Marshal Long," he explained, reaching into his pocket and retrieving his badge so they could see that he was telling the truth. "A few moments ago, I was forced to kill two men and badly injured a third."

"We heard the gunshots," one of the men said. "You killed *two* men?"

"I had no choice. Now, I wonder if you would be so kind as to escort my lady back to her home. I have to take care of this business and she finds it very upsetting."

"Small wonder!" one of the women said. "What on earth happened?"

"They wanted to rob and abuse us," Longarm explained. "I really would appreciate it if you would escort the young lady back to her home. It isn't far and we'd both be in your debt."

"Of course we will!" one of the men proclaimed. "No woman should have to look upon such a terrible sight!"

"My sentiments exactly," Longarm told the gentleman. "And I might suggest that in the future, you people do not walk unarmed in this area."

"You can be sure of that."

Longarm knew that Lucy McCoy was upset, and he wished he could have taken the time to calm her fears, but that just wasn't possible. There were two dead bodies to report to the local authorities, as well as a third man who required immediate attention.

"I . . . I want you to stop by and see me," Lucy said a few minutes later. "When you have finished with this awful business, come by and hold me a little while. Will you please do that, Custis?"

He could feel that she was still trembling. "Of course. It shouldn't take me more than an hour to wrap this up. Lucy, I'm sorry about what just happened."

"It's not *your* fault." Lucy threw her arms around Custis's neck and hugged him tightly. "Oh, dear heavens, whatever would have happened to me if I'd been with poor, sweet Robert!"

"Who is *Robert*?"

"He's one of my father's youngest and most promising bank officers. But never mind him. You're the one I know that I can always count on."

"I'll be along as soon as I can," Longarm said, kissing her lips. "Shall I just knock on the front door of your family's house or . . ."

"You know where my bedroom is. The window will be unlocked."

"You want me to come into your bedroom with your parents sleeping not thirty feet away in the next room?"

"Yes, I don't want to be alone tonight."

"All right."

Lucy kissed him hard before he handed her over to the care of the two couples, asking, "Are you gentlemen armed?"

"No," both men replied in unison.

Longarm returned to the dead gunman's body. He pried a good Colt revolver from the man's stiffening fingers, then offered it to the more vigorous of the two men, saying, "The man I killed won't need this anymore, and you should carry it whenever you go out in the city after dark. We do our best to keep the streets safe, but we can't cover everything, now can we?"

"Why, of course not."

Longarm turned and headed back to the man he'd beaten. "On your feet!"

The man was lying on his side clutching his privates. When Longarm dragged him erect, he cried out, but Longarm had little sympathy. "Quit your whining. You're still alive, aren't you?"

"Who . . . who are you?"

"Deputy Marshal Custis Long."

The man whimpered like a beaten puppy as Longarm shoved him up the street toward the nearest jail cell. "Mister," Longarm said, "you and your friends sure did your best to mess up my evening!"

He'd taken the knife-wielding thief to the nearest police station, made sure that the man was booked for attempted murder, then hurried back across town to one of the wealthiest neighborhoods in town.

Remembering Lucy's instructions, Longarm rapped lightly on her bedroom window. She must have been sitting beside it because Lucy raised the window almost at once.

"How are you?" he asked.

She was wearing a lacy pink nightgown and looked like

21

an angel. "Oh, Custis, I'm still shaking. I've never seen anyone die before or so much blood!" Lucy shuddered and hugged herself, exposing a portion of the soft mounds of her luscious breast. "It was awful!"

It was all he could do to keep from staring. "I'm really sorry that I didn't drill him through the heart like I did the first one. But I just shot a little bit high, that's all."

"He died so—"

"Lucy, you can't be thinking of that, so just try to push it out of your mind forever. Those men would have robbed and killed me without giving it a second thought. And they'd have done even worse things to you."

"I know. Come inside."

Longarm climbed through the window, and Lucy rushed into his arms, breathing into his ear, "Please hold me tight for a while."

"Uh . . . it'd be more comfortable on the bed."

She nodded, and they sat down on the edge of Lucy's bed. Longarm held the young woman for perhaps an hour, and then his shoulders and lower back started to tighten, so he kicked off his boots, removed his coat, and stretched out on her bed.

"Might as well be comfortable."

"Might as well," Lucy agreed, lying down beside him. "But I'm not sure what Mother or Father would think of this."

"I'm a United States Marshal and a Southern gentleman."

"You *were* a Southern gentleman."

"Oh, I still am, Lucy. I just take my time with things and let them run their natural course."

"Meaning?"

"Meaning that here we are after a terrible ordeal, still safe and sound. I've always thought that a crisis brings people closer together . . . provided they survive."

"Oh, really?"

"Sure." Longarm leaned over and placed his hand on Lucy's breast, which yielded so nicely to his fingertips. "Now let's talk about you and me."

She pushed his hand aside, but when he kissed her, she clung to him as if she were still out on the street and her life was in jeopardy. "I was so afraid, and you were so brave and cool-headed!" she breathed as his hand came back to rest where it had been only a moment before, and then began to move in a light brushing and circular motion that caused Lucy to shiver.

"Custis, I don't think any other man alive could have saved me from those . . . those animals!"

"Probably not," he agreed, hand on the move again.

Lucy was so upset that she either didn't care or notice where his hand stopped. That was fine with Longarm. She was soft, sweet, and he was eager to show her the ways of love . . . given this rare opportunity.

"Custis, we've only known each other for a week."

"That's right, but it seems a lot longer, doesn't it?"

"Oh, yes! You know, when I told Father and Mother that you were a lawman, they were shocked and . . . I'm ashamed to say, upset."

Longarm kissed her lips softly. "I thought that I wouldn't quite meet their standards."

"It's not that they're bigheaded or stuffy."

His fingers slid lightly up her thigh and she shivered uncontrollably. When she began to resist, he kissed her again, more passionately this time, and she wound her arms around him tight.

"What are you doing?" she breathed.

"I'm doing what you think I'm doing."

"Oh. Oh, my!"

Longarm reached far up under her nightgown, and when his fingers touched that soft, forbidden place, he felt her wetness. "Lucy, I think we ought to get even more comfortable and get undressed."

23

"You're going to make love to me, aren't you?"

"That's the idea."

"Oh, dear! And I've been saving myself all this time for Robert."

"Let's not talk about Robert," Longarm said, sitting up and quickly undressing. "If he's waited this long, he might not be the man you want to marry."

"He's so . . . so different from you. He makes a lot of money and my father said that someday he'll take over our bank, but—"

Longarm crushed her lips into silence, and then he pushed the lacy pink nightgown up over her hips and gently spread her legs. "Lucy," he whispered, "am I your first man?"

"No."

"What!"

"Shhh! Not so loud. I've had men before, for heaven's sakes! I'm twenty-one years old."

"Yeah, but what about Robert?"

"He is . . . different."

"Well, I'm not!" Longarm eased his massive rod into her wet womanhood, and when she shuddered and moaned, he began to rotate his hips slowly.

"Oh, my heavens," Lucy groaned, "you're not like anybody I've ever had."

"Have you had a lot of men?"

"Boys," she breathed. "Until now, I thought they were men . . . but they were just boys."

Longarm smiled and kept kissing her. Pretty soon, Lucy locked her legs around his plunging hips and they both started slamming up and down on the mattress.

"Holy cow!" Lucy cried. "This is wonderful!"

"Shhh!" he pleaded.

But his pleas were in vain, and when their bodies lost control and Longarm began to spew torrents of his hot seed into Lucy, she threw her head back and cried out with pleasure.

Moments later, there was a loud knocking on the door. "Lucy! Lucy what is going on in there?"

"It's Father!" she whispered, pushing Longarm aside and leaping off the bed.

"I'm fine, Father!"

"Open up. What's going on in there! Robert? Are you in there with my daughter? I'll get a gun, Robert! You were supposed to wait! You promised Mrs. McCoy and myself you would wait!"

Longarm heard the man stomping off into another room.

"Is he really getting a gun?"

"Yes!"

Longarm grabbed his pants, shirt, boots, and coat, then his gunbelt, and dove through the window. He landed on damp grass, jumped up, and frantically began to dress.

"Oh, Custis, come back tomorrow night!" she begged, hanging half out the window.

My, oh, my, but she was a beauty. But when he heard more pounding on Lucy's door, he said, "Not unless you promise to let me gag you before we do it again!"

"Anything! Just come back tomorrow night!"

Longarm heard wood splinter. Lucy disappeared, slamming shut her window, and Longarm, still only half dressed, took off down the street running.

Chapter 3

"Custis," Billy Vail snapped the next morning, "what the hell happened to you last night!"

"What do you mean?" Longarm asked, trying to stifle a yawn.

"I mean you killed two men and almost ruined a third. I've already had a visit from the local authorities wanting to know exactly what you did out there last night."

Longarm took a deep breath and expelled it slowly. He'd only gotten a couple of hours of sleep, and was in no mood to be harangued. "The truth of the matter is that I was set upon by three men who had murder and rape on their minds."

"I should have known you were with a woman."

"A lady friend and I were at the park down by Cherry Creek when these three men threatened us with a gun and knives. I was pretty lucky to get out of there with my life."

"And the young lady?"

"She was very upset, as you'd expect."

"The locals are going to want a full report. Apparently, you did little more than drop the sole survivor off at the jail last night without even bothering to give your name."

"They know me well."

"I'm sure they do," Billy said. "Considering that you seem to get into more trouble than any five of my other deputy marshals combined."

"Look, I rid Denver of some very bad characters. Now, what else do we have to talk about this morning?"

"The Love Sisters."

"Last night I could have used the help of . . . what was her name?"

"You'd be talking about Big Mamma. And it is funny that you should mention her because she has arrived here ahead of the other ladies and I want you to meet her this afternoon." Billy frowned. "Custis, I haven't met the woman myself, but from what I've heard, she can be . . . difficult."

"You already told me that she was a heller who could shoot and fight like a man."

"I've been warned that she can also cuss and intimidate men. That's one of the reasons you were our first and nearly only choice for this job."

"Billy, I'm not going to be pushed around by any woman no matter how big and tough."

"Of course not. We'd never expect you to bend and scrape, but for this mission of mercy to be successful, you will have to be accommodating. Not only to Big Mamma, but to the other women."

Longarm didn't like the way this conversation was traveling, and began to pace back and forth, trying to put into words where he would draw his own line in the sand.

"Listen to me, Billy. I'm only doing this because you are a dear friend and hired me for this job."

"And for six weeks paid vacation. Director Cardiff was not too pleased about that concession."

"But he agreed to it. Right?"

"Yeah," Billy said, "he did. But I wouldn't try to collect on it if something goes wrong on this assignment. The

Love Sisters will be a big story when they return back East, and their experience in Colorado had better be good."

"Don't lay it all on my shoulders. I'm just their wrangler and mystery protector. Remember?"

"Why don't you go see the local authorities and tell them what they need to know for their reports. That man that you arrested last night is in damn poor shape."

"He's lucky just to be alive."

"They may want to have the girl you were with also file a report. After all, two men were killed."

"What girl?" Longarm asked on his way out the door.

"Custis, there are rules and even you have to follow them sometimes!" Billy shouted after Longarm.

"Yeah. Yeah."

Longarm had an unpleasant hour with the local authorities answering their questions about the two dead men and the one that he'd arrested. Denver Sergeant Homer Bartlett was new at his job and trying to make a good impression. He was extremely fat and a stickler for irrelevant details. In Longarm's opinion, Bartlett seemed more interested in covering his behind than in taking dangerous criminals off his streets.

They got off to a rocky start when Bartlett said, "I don't much appreciate you federal lawmen taking on a gunslinger mentality in my city."

" 'Gunslinger'?" Longarm snorted with disgust. "Sergeant, maybe you haven't cleaned your ears out in a few months. Those three men were going to kill me!"

"Were there any witnesses to what you've told us so far?"

"Not a one," Longarm lied.

"That's not what the fella you brought in said."

"Oh?"

"He tells me there was a woman!"

28

"Hmm." Longarm looked puzzled. "There might have been. You know, Sergeant, everything happened so damned fast that I just sort of disremember."

"Horseshit! You're not telling us the whole truth. I can see that as plain as the wart on my hand. And I may have to go to your superior and tell him that you aren't willing to cooperate."

"His name is Marshal Billy Vail and his boss's name is Director George Cardiff. They're a couple of nice fellas and they'll speak highly of me, Sergeant."

"Humph! Like I said, I don't appreciate your high-and-mighty attitude. You can't shoot up my city, kill two men, and then drop off a third without filling out the proper reports."

"Sergeant, I'm illiterate. That's why I didn't fill them out."

"He's lying," another officer said. "He wrote down his name last night."

"Oh, sure," Longarm said, "I can write my name. But that's all."

"Oh, horseshit!" Sergeant Bartlett screamed.

"You shouldn't get so upset," Longarm said calmly. "A man of your size could have his heart seize up. I've seen it happen to fat men before, and I remember one that had the whole side of his face freeze so that when he ate—"

"Shut up!"

"Are we finished here?" Longarm asked. "Because I do have work of my own waiting back at the office."

"Don't let me see you here again, and stay close by. We'll want you to testify when the surviving attacker goes before a court."

"You know where to find me," Longarm told the man as he climbed out of his chair to head back to his office.

Bartlett flew into a rage. "Mister, you ain't Wild Bill Hickok and this isn't Abilene, Kansas!"

"True enough, Homer. But *you* ain't Wyatt Earp and this isn't Tombstone."

Longarm went back to his room and slept for several hours. When he awoke, he bathed, shaved, and returned to the Federal Building a little before three o'clock that afternoon.

"They're waiting for you in the Director's office," Marshal Weaver warned. "And wait until you see Big Mamma!"

"Pretty impressive, huh?"

"I sure wouldn't want her mad at me, but she is a looker. Woo-wee! That is a big hunk of gorgeous woman! Every man in the building is talking about her. I'm beginning to think that you are the lucky one to have gotten this assignment."

"I thought you were supposed to be on your way to Montana to stop a range war."

"Oh, I am. But the train is running a few hours late. I'll be on it later."

"Good luck."

"Same to you," Weaver remarked as Longarm headed for the Director's office.

When he knocked, Billy Vail opened the door with a wide grin on his chubby face. "Custis, you look good."

"Thanks," he replied.

"Clean-shaven, washed, and everything. Come on in!"

When Longarm laid eyes on Big Mamma, he was brought up short in his tracks. The woman was as tall as himself, with wide shoulders, large bosom, and shapely hips. She wore a dress, but seemed better suited to wearing pants. Not that she wasn't a lovely woman, but she just seemed too big for women's clothes.

"Marshal Custis Long, I presume," she said, coming toward him with an outstretched hand.

"That's right." When they shook, he felt the power of her grip. Too much power. And she studied him in a way that made Longarm feel as if she was taking his measure and finding him wanting in some way or another.

"My name is Mrs. Georgia O'Grady," she said. "I was married to a wonderful Irish fighter named Shamus O'Grady. After he died, some of his ex-pugilist friends who had relied upon Shamus for . . . shall we say, his generosity . . . began to call me Big Mamma when I continued to give them support. I don't give them much, but they need only a little to survive. Some of them were permanently damaged in the ring. My house has become a refuge for some of those wonderful men."

"What," Longarm asked, "was your husband's cause of death?"

"Shamus was to fight Paddy Ryan for the championship. The title fight was to be held in Boston, but there were those that were afraid Shamus would win . . . and he likely would have had he not been poisoned on the train from New York, where we live."

"Poisoned?" Billy Vail asked.

"That's right. He died in agony on the train. Later, they arrested and convicted the murderer, and I am happy to say that Paddy Ryan had no knowledge of the man or his act. It was simply a fan who loved Paddy and could not bear the idea that he might lose his title, which he has already done to John L. Sullivan."

"Yes, I knew that," Longarm said.

"Well, I was devastated," Big Mamma said with tears in her eyes. "Shamus O'Grady had a heart of gold and fists of iron. He could have beat Paddy Ryan and John L. Sullivan at the same time!"

"What a shame," Billy Vail lamented.

"Yes, it was. Shamus and I first met in a circus where I was a . . . strong lady. I used to perform feats of strength in a little tent and arm-wrestle men for prizes. I almost never lost. There is a skill to arm-wrestling, just as there is to fighting, you know. Shamus taught me both and much more."

"Like how to shoot?"

"Ah," Big Mamma said, "so you've heard of that, have you?"

"Yes."

"Well, Shamus was a terrible shot. I learned to do that from my own dear father, God rest his soul. My father was a crack shot and since I was his only child, he had no choice but to treat me like the son he always wanted. So I learned some manly things even before I ran off with the circus and later met Shamus."

"You've done a lot of living in a very few years," Longarm said.

"Marshal, how old do you think I am?"

Longarm knew from experience that this was a question a man never answered without subtracting a good many years off a woman's age to be on the safe side. "Oh, about twenty-two, I should think."

"I'm almost twenty-five and you are . . . a true gentleman. But are you much of a fighter, Mr. Long?"

"I win some and I've lost a few."

Billy cleared his throat. "Custis is too modest. He's the best man we have to put in the field. He's killed . . . what . . . fifteen men?"

"A few more," Longarm replied.

"Oh, yes, I forgot that you added to your total just last night."

"Yes," Director Cardiff said. "And I've got to soothe some feathers later today with the local authorities. Marshal, you really should—"

"Who'd you kill?" Big Mamma interrupted, looking intently at Longarm.

"No one important. Just a couple of vicious robbers."

"What happened?"

Longarm quickly told her how the three men had drawn

32

their weapons and accosted himself and a young lady, and what had happened as a result. He even pulled out his pocket watch and showed Big Mamma how one end of his watch chain led to a two-shot derringer.

"Very clever. But you should have killed that third fellow," Big Mamma advised. "That man will someday be released from prison, and he just might happen to see you walking down the street. If he sees you first, he could decide to kill you."

"That is a risk any officer of the law takes," Longarm told her. "On the other hand, he might remember what happened the first time we met. If he does, he'll likely shit his britches and run like a rabbit."

Big Mamma brayed with laughter. Finally, she caught her breath and said, "You are every bit as confident as I am and I really appreciate that."

"I like my own odds when the going gets rough, if that's what you mean."

"I think you and me are going to get along just fine."

"So do I," Longarm agreed.

"Just remember that *I'll* be in charge of the Love Sisters. You'll be in charge of the horses and making sure that we have suitable room accommodations, and that we aren't harassed by drunken miners or anyone else that's into their cups and is thinking that they want to have some fun with one of the Love Sisters."

"How many will there be?"

"Me and six others."

"The heavenly Seven Sisters, huh?"

"That's right." Big Mamma winked. "So, Marshal, you have a rudimentary understanding of constellations and astronomy."

"I like to look at the stars and try to find things."

"I'll just bet you do, and never alone or in the company of men. Right?"

Longarm ignored the question. "When do I meet them?"

"Tomorrow, and we'll leave at once."

"You're not giving them any time to rest up in Denver after that long train ride from the East?"

"No." Big Mamma took a chair. She looked up at everyone in the room and said, "It's only fair that I tell you that these ladies are rich, idealistic . . . and spoiled rotten. They've all been born with a silver spoon and not one of them has ever had a moment of hardship. One of the reasons why I want to leave tomorrow is that I don't want the Love Sisters to quickly become known as the Weak Sisters. Now I am sure that when I announce we'll leave on a wagon the very same day that they arrive . . . several will quit."

"Quit?" Director Cardiff asked with surprise. "Why, that wouldn't look good in the newspapers."

"Hang the damned newspapers!"

"But what about the President's granddaughter and his interest in this 'mission of mercy'?"

Big Mamma pointed a finger at the ceiling. "Ah, you'd be talking about Miss Alice Fairchild! Oh, yes, dear Alice. Now we should talk about her for a moment."

"I think we should," Longarm agreed, sensing he was about to learn something unpleasant.

"Miss Fairchild is a 'fair child.' She is young and lovely, with long blond locks and rosy red cheeks. She looks like a fairy-tale princess . . . but she isn't." Big Mamma glanced at the door to make sure it was closed. When she turned back to speak, she lowered her voice and said, "Gentlemen, I want your words that whatever I say in this room stays in this room."

"By all means!" Director Cardiff emphatically promised. "You have our words on that."

"Right," Billy Vail seconded.

"Fine by me," Longarm told the huge woman, who was actually starting to appeal to him.

Big Mamma leaned back in her chair and crossed her legs like a man showing more than her ankle. "All right then, Miss Alice Fairchild is, in reality, a slut."

"No!" the Director gasped.

"It's true. She has become an embarrassment to the entire Presidential family. The girl gets into one amour after another. It is a miracle that she has not yet had a child out of wedlock. Furthermore, she is arrogant, spoiled, and completely self-centered and selfish."

Big Mamma sighed. "Custis, I don't expect you to believe this. I'd prefer that you didn't and just watched Alice and made up your own mind. But the truth is, the girl is a troublemaker and a man-hunter. Your number-one job will be to keep her from getting pregnant."

"Oh, now wait a minute here!"

"I'm sorry," Big Mamma told him. "And the worst part is that several of the other young ladies aren't much better than Alice Fairchild. They are a bunch of prima donnas who came up with this . . . this idea on a whim and out of a sense of boredom. If they can last it out, they'll return to the East as famous as celebrities. They will have accomplished something far greater than they have ever done before."

"This," Billy Vail said, "is very sobering."

"Yes," Big Mamma said, "that's what I thought after I was pulled into this affair and asked to become a Love Sister. Custis, if we don't watch them like hawks, they will all become Love Sisters in *every* sense of the word."

"Why are you doing this?" Longarm asked.

"They are paying me five thousand dollars."

"That's it?"

"No," the big woman said, "it isn't. You see, they will have the authority to grant charity to mining women. There is a large fund that has accumulated and it will be our job, as Love Sisters, to decide who gets how much. I think that this money can make a huge difference and greatly assist some women who might otherwise die young and in poverty. It will also help any children that they have. To me, that is the most important reason for my being a Love Sister."

"But five thousand helps," Longarm said.

"Of course it does. As I explained earlier, after my husband was poisoned, several of his old boxing friends who were in desperate circumstances turned to me in their need. I want to be able to continue to help them. Five thousand dollars will go a long, long way toward that end. I even have a few younger fighters who I might manage in hope of a good return on my investment."

"You are both good-hearted and a woman with an eye to the future," Longarm said. "It will be a pleasure to help you all that I can."

"But this could blow up in all our faces," Big Mamma warned. "I don't get paid unless the Love Sisters can be judged a success."

Longarm nodded with understanding. Compared to Big Mamma's reasons for helping, his own request for six weeks of paid vacation seemed unimportant even to the point of being trivial.

"What time shall we meet tomorrow?" Longarm asked the woman.

"Let's meet at the train station in a stagecoach pulled by at least four horses."

"Four horses?"

"The Love Sisters," Big Mamma explained, "do not travel lightly. They have quite a few trunks. Also, it would not do to have their pretty faces exposed to the elements."

"If Longarm is driving," Billy Vail said, "I think he needs a shotgun rider."

"That won't be necessary," Big Mamma told him. "I'll ride up on top with a rifle, dressed in a man's clothing."

36

Director Cardiff started to object. "Miss O'Grady, I don't think that you realize the danger. Someone could mistake your coach and think it carries something very valuable."

"That would be no mistake, sir."

"Yes, I understand, but . . ."

Big Mamma turned to Longarm, ignoring the Director. "Marshal Long, let's meet here at noon and drive the coach over to the train station. I don't believe that your local newspapers have gotten wind of the arrival of the Love Sisters. At least, we've tried very hard to prevent that. But just in case they have, let us be ready to roll for the mining camps on the moment."

"That's fine. I'll be down in the street and have everything ready."

"You might stock a supply of champagne and some chocolates."

Longarm blinked. "I beg your pardon?"

"Oh, never mind," Big Mamma said. "Just be ready to roll."

"Count on me," Longarm promised. "Is the meeting over?"

"I believe so," Director Cardiff said, "unless Miss O'Grady has something else to tell us?"

"No," she replied. "I had thought that we might have dinner together tonight."

"Why, of course!" Cardiff exclaimed. "Why didn't I—"

"I meant a dinner with Marshal Long and myself could prove worthwhile."

Longarm and Big Mamma's eyes locked for an instant, and he wondered if what he saw in the woman was what he thought he saw. Oh, probably not. Big Mamma was all business, and besides, he had already promised to pay a lusty farewell visit to Lucy McCoy, providing her rich banker father hadn't chained her to the fireplace.

Chapter 4

It was eleven o'clock at night and the lights in the McCoy residence had all been extinguished at least an hour earlier. Satisfied that everything was as it should be, Longarm moved silently across the front lawn and tapped lightly on Lucy's window. "Honey, it's me!" he whispered.

The window opened at once and Longarm climbed inside, eager for what promised to be a very vigorous and unforgettable night of farewell. But no sooner did he gain full entry to Lucy's bedroom than he heard the cocking of a pistol.

"Custis, run!" Lucy cried from another room.

Longarm didn't have to be told twice. He pivoted and dove back through the window just as a gun exploded twice. Longarm howled as a bullet dug a deep, nasty furrow across both of his buttocks. He struck the ground and vaulted to his feet, one hand on his burning buttocks as he sprinted back out to the street, making a sharp turn on the corner and running like the devil.

He did not stop until he was several blocks away, and then he bent over and gingerly touched his butt cheeks, grimacing with pain. "Damn!"

Longarm limped home and inspected himself as well as he possibly could. The good news was that Mr. McCoy's bullet had only sliced a nasty flesh wound across both cheeks and there was no bullet to remove. The bad news was that he was losing considerable blood, had ruined his pants, and was going to be in severe pain for a good long while.

"Damn," he muttered again as he attempted to first clean the awful wound and then apply a bandage.

He couldn't fall asleep until about two o'clock in the morning, and then only with the aid of a considerable amount of whiskey to assuage his flesh and dignity.

What am I going to do about tomorrow? he wondered. How can I possibly manage to hide the fact that I have been grievously wounded in an unspeakable part of my anatomy? I'm going to have to hide it somehow or I'll be the laughingstock of Denver.

Longarm had some laudanum in his medicine cabinet. He'd put the strong pain medication to good use a number of times, but his stock was running low. Well, tomorrow morning, despite his busy schedule, he was determined to find the time to replenish his supply. With a full bottle of the painkiller, he could just tough it out until the wound healed enough so that his injury didn't cause him to limp or wince.

But he overslept the next morning, and by the time he figured out a way to prevent the bandage from slipping off his posterior and then down his leg, it was almost ten o'clock. Worse still, the only thing that seemed to work was a sort of makeshift diaper. Just taping a bandage across his buttocks simply invited disaster.

Longarm was irritable and running late when he finally got to the livery stable and explained his needs to the proprietor, Danny Rankin. "Marshal Long, do you even know how to drive a four-horse team?"

"Of course I do!"

"And hitch as well as unhitch them?"

"I might need a few pointers," Longarm conceded. "It's been quite some time since I did that."

"All right," Rankin said with a knowing smile, "you watch and I'll go through it slow. By the way, who is so bloody important that you have to escort 'em in a stagecoach?"

"Never you mind," Longarm told the young stable owner.

"Are they coming in on today's train?"

"Let's quit jawin' because I'm short of time. Just show me how to hitch up the team," Longarm growled.

"Sure, Marshal, but the thing I most want to know is how come you're walking kinda funny and up on your toes?"

"Danny, get the horses and hitch them to this coach!"

The stagecoach itself was all dirty and dusty. There were rats' nests in the seats and cobwebs everywhere.

"How long has it been since you rented this monster out?" Longarm asked.

"A couple years."

"Is it in running order?"

"I'll put some grease on the axles and it'll be fine."

"It better be," Longarm said, "or not only won't you get paid, but I'll come back and give you hell."

"Yes, sir," Danny said, not looking too worried.

It took both men the remainder of the morning to clean the stagecoach properly and grease the axles. By then, there was no time to get the laudanum, and Longarm was in considerable pain.

"Marshal, you look sorta pasty-faced," the liveryman fretted. "You got a boil on your ass or something?"

"Or something. Are we finally ready to roll?"

"Yes, sir. You paying me or is the government?"

"Bill 'em as usual," Longarm told the young man. "And bill 'em high."

"I'll charge 'em ten dollars a day for the team of horses and another ten for the stagecoach and harness. How long will you be needing them?"

"Two weeks at the most."

"Take your time and don't hurry. At twenty dollars a day, a man could build up his retirement."

"Help me up into the seat, will you?"

Danny gave Longarm a curious look, then a boost. "The seat of your pants is all bumpy. What—"

"See ya in two weeks or less, if I get lucky," Longarm said as he slapped the reins down hard on the rumps of the wheel horses. The animals jumped forward, throwing Longarm back hard onto the seat.

"Uhhh, dammit!" he groaned as he drove the stagecoach down toward Colfax and the Federal Building.

Big Mamma was waiting in front of the Federal Building when Longarm pulled the stage up and managed a thin smile.

"What happened to you?" she asked, looking up at him.

"What do you mean?"

"You look awful this morning."

"I . . . I didn't sleep too well."

"Oh."

Big Mamma had told him she was going to be wearing a man's shirt and pants and ride shotgun, and she hadn't been kidding. Longarm couldn't help but stare. At first glance, and because of her height and size, you thought the woman was a mighty fine specimen of manhood. But then you looked closer and realized that Mrs. Georgia O'Grady was a woman, and quite a shapely and attractive one at that. She had long, long legs and her hips weren't too big and broad. The big leather coat she wore tried but failed to hide the fact that she was extremely well endowed. Big Mamma's hair was dark brown, but now it was hidden under a slouch hat.

41

"I'll come down and help you up," Longarm reluctantly offered.

"Don't bother," she said, sparing him the agony as she handed him a new Winchester rifle. "I can get up there just fine."

And she did. Big Mamma's long legs made climbing up to the driver's seat look easy. Once she was seated beside him, she said, "Custis, mind telling me what happened to you last night?"

"What do you mean?"

"I mean you look like hell." She leaned close and sniffed at his breath. "Are you a drunkard?"

"Hell, no!"

"That's a relief. The only thing I have against some of my husband's old Irish fighters is they tipple a bit too much. Are you Irish?"

"Some, maybe."

"I expect we all have a bit of Irish in our blood. I do, but not much. Without a little Irish, we often take ourselves far too seriously. Know what I mean?"

"Sure." Longarm drove on down the street toward the train depot. The traffic was heavy and there were a lot of buggies and carriages going in the same direction. It all meant that he'd have to walk a fair distance to greet the Love Sisters, and that wasn't a pleasant prospect, given his unusual infirmity.

"That's the thing I've noticed about the rich," Big Mamma was saying.

Longarm glanced aside at her. "What's that?"

"They don't have enough Irish in 'em and take themselves way too seriously. Now, these girls are like that. They believe the sun rises and sets for them alone. I am telling you this, Custis, so that you will be prepared for what you are about to face. These girls do have their good points . . . a lot of them, in fact . . . but they are demanding."

42

"There's not much they can demand where we're headed."

"I hope not. Your boss told me that you aren't married. That was essential. If a handsome dog like you were married, I wouldn't have allowed you to come along because it'd be too hard."

"Meaning that the Love Sisters are irresistible?"

"I think they would be for the average workingman. These girls are pretty, but you couple that with all their money, and I think it would be an overpowering temptation for a married man."

Longarm was amused. "So how do you think I'm going to handle this situation?"

"I am confident you will handle it well," Big Mamma said without hesitation. "I did some careful checking on your background. You have a reputation as a ladies' man."

"Now, whoever told you that!"

"Don't try to pull my leg," Big Mamma told him. "You *are* a ladies' man, but that is the only kind that could handle these girls. You take a shy fella, he'd be fodder for the Love Sisters because they'd delight in teasing him half to death. And you take a fool or a braggart, they'd also find ways to chop him down to size. I told Director Cardiff that I needed a man who had confidence in himself, but also enough self-restraint not to jump into the honey pot . . . if you know what I mean."

"I do."

"Don't get involved with them," Big Mamma warned. "You'll have your chances, but don't do it."

"They're of age, aren't they?"

"Sure, and a couple of them would be easy pickings for a man like you. But what I'm saying is that you have a sworn duty to uphold their honor."

"Even if one or two decide they don't want their honor upheld?"

"That's right. I expect these girls are going to be pretty easy to impress, despite all their money and sophistication. Starting with yourself, a lot of the rugged Western men are going to make some of their back-home beaus seem bloodless by comparison. You know what I'm saying?"

"I believe so."

Big Mamma grabbed his arm and squeezed it hard. "Custis, remember that even though you are not supposed to be a marshal to those we meet, you are still bound by oath to do your job with honor. And the honorable thing is not to take advantage of what might seem like easy pickings."

"I won't."

"Your word on it?"

"If I prove too irresistible to one of 'em, I'll just do something kinda rank and that will change their mind."

"Rank like what?"

"Pick my nose. Scratch my balls. Fart loud enough to send crows flying out of the treetops. Something like that."

She laughed. "I think we are going to make a good pair of watchdogs."

"I think so too," he said, meaning it.

They had to leave the coach quite some distance from the train depot and make their way through the crowded assembly of wagons in order to get to the passenger loading platform. The train rolled in about a half hour late as usual, and the Love Sisters were the very last ones to disembark.

The first girl was willowy, with red hair, green eyes, and a tentative smile. She was quite attractive in a fragile sort of way.

"That is Martha."

"Last name?"

"We're not using last names," Big Mamma told him. "And the brunette behind her is Cassandra. She is going to be very difficult."

"How so?"

"Cassie loves the spotlight. She's constantly seeking attention. And the short, perky girl is Linda."

"Cute."

"She thinks so too." Big Mamma stayed out of sight as the girls appeared one by one. "That blonde is named Elizabeth. She is smart as anything, but uses her intelligence to outwit men. She makes a game of that, in fact, and you must watch out or she will wind up pulling your leg without you having a clue."

"Thanks for the warning."

"The next is Milly."

Milly had black hair and a beautiful yellow dress. She looked like an angel. "What's her fault?" he asked.

"I haven't figured Milly out yet. Perhaps she is as innocent and perfect as she appears. Milly is probably also the wealthiest, and she seems to have a quality that sets her slightly apart from the others. I have high hopes for that one."

"Where is Alice Fairchild?"

"She'll be along. Alice prefers to *stage* her entrance."

"At a dinky place like this train station?" Longarm asked with surprise.

"Anywhere. But don't call her Miss Fairchild. She is to be addressed only as Miss Alice. Heaven forbid some reporter makes the connection that she is the granddaughter of the President of these United States."

"Of course."

"Ah," Big Mamma said, "there is dear, spoiled-rotten Alice."

Longarm shook his head when Alice sort of floated down from the train. She was quite beautiful, tall and graceful, with soft, curly brown hair that cascaded to her shoulders. She exuded wealth and privilege and gave the impression of being a Southern belle, though Longarm knew all these girls were from wealthy Northern families.

"She could turn the head of any man," he said.

"And she knows it," Big Mamma said as the six Love Sisters began to mill around and every man present turned to stare at the unusual bevy of lovely young ladies.

"Well, I think we had better go to the rescue before they are mobbed."

"I agree. You go back to the stagecoach and pull your hat down low. What I want to do is have them board quickly and without making any more of a scene than is necessary. We'll head for . . . where?"

"We'll stop at a way station on the way up to the little mining town of Gold Creek," Longarm answered. "It's only a four-hour trip up into the Rockies. I know a good rooming house where you can all eat and sleep peacefully. It's a place where you won't attract a lot of attention."

"Then it's a good choice," Big Mamma said as she hurried off to greet the six young women, who were being surrounded by men eager to help carry their baggage and make their immediate acquaintance.

Longarm returned to the coach, struggled up into the seat, and pulled his hat down low over his face. He did not want to be recognized either. Not with this kind of a job on his hands.

It seemed to take the Love Sisters an awfully long time to arrive at the stagecoach. Longarm didn't greet them, nor did he look up so they could see his face. He just sat huddled in the driver's box and listened to the Love Sisters complain about the long train ride and the terrible accommodations they'd had to suffer coming out from the East.

"I know, I know," Big Mamma kept repeating. "It's terrible what a lady has to endure out in the West. But

46

we have to be strong and remember that the mining women we've come to help are so much more in need of assistance than ourselves."

"Yes, but where are we going now?" a Love Sister asked, sounding peevish.

"Oh," Big Mamma answered, "we are going up into those beautiful mountains for the night."

"You mean to tell me that we're not staying here in Denver tonight?" she cried. "You mean we get off that horrible train and have to climb into this awful stagecoach right now?"

"I'm afraid so, Cassie. But it won't be so awful."

"You look ridiculous dressed up like a man. Why are you dressed like that?"

"Because I'm going to be riding shotgun on top with the driver."

"What is that?"

"It's nothing, dear Linda."

"But—"

"Don't fret about it," Big Mamma assured the girl.

"Who's the big man driving us?"

"He's nobody. Now, girls, hurry up and get inside so that we can leave for the hotel."

Hotel? Longarm thought. They would be staying in a mountain way station.

"And," Big Mamma added, "porters, please hoist the baggage into the rear boot and tie everything down securely. We don't want anything to fall out, now do we?"

It took the whining Love Sisters nearly fifteen minutes to get their baggage arranged to their satisfaction and then to take their places inside. Longarm had never heard so much griping in his life.

"This coach is filthy!"

"My dress is already ruined."

"Back home I would *never* ride in such a wreck as this.

47

Disgusting! Can't we find a better means of transportation!"

"I'm afraid not," Big Mamma said, sounding solicitous. "And I know it is quite awful, but we can't arrive in the mining camps in a golden carriage, now can we? How would that look to the poor women we come to assist? And remember that we are supposed to be some kind of traveling troupe of entertainers."

"I can sing beautifully."

"I'm sure that you can, Alice. What about you other ladies?"

Longarm listened, and gathered that they all thought they were pretty accomplished singers. He lit a cigar, took a slug of laudanum mixed with whiskey from a bottle in his coat pocket, and tried not to think about the next couple of weeks in what was already becoming an ongoing nightmare.

Chapter 5

When Big Mamma swung up on the seat beside him, Longarm gave her a disgusted look and said, "We're in for a hell of a time these next two weeks."

"That's right."

Longarm flicked the lines, slapping the rumps of the two near horses. The animals jumped, which suddenly jerked the stagecoach forward. Longarm was thrown back hard on his haunches, and it hurt like blazes, but the pain was offset by the satisfaction he received when he heard the Love Sisters squeal with displeasure.

"What the devil is wrong with you!" Big Mamma demanded.

It was all Longarm could do to keep from grinning as he said, "Not a single thing."

"You'd better learn to start a team up easier than that, or those girls will be after me to fire you."

"Sorry," he said, though he really wasn't.

They drove through the crowded streets of Denver, headed west up the main road past the high buttes, and started into the mountains.

"Hey," one of the Love Sisters shouted, "we need to stop!"

"What's their problem now?" Longarm asked.

"They have to have relieve themselves," Big Mamma said.

Longarm stared at the woman. "Why didn't they do that just before they got off the train?"

"Because they aren't in the habit of thinking ahead about these sorts of natural emergencies. But they'll get better. Now pull over and they can visit that stand of trees."

"Yes, ma'am," Longarm replied, easing the team to the side of the steep, winding road.

The moment he stopped the coach, the women piled out, and several actually gave Longarm dirty looks as if it were *his* fault that they would have to resort to such primitive measures.

"When are we going to get to wherever it is we are going?" Alice Fairchild demanded to know.

Big Mamma shrugged. "You'll have to ask our driver. I've never been to Colorado either."

Alice studied Longarm as if he were a cockroach. "Well?"

"It'll be about ten more miles."

"How long will *that* take?"

"About three more hours. It's all uphill climbing and this is a heavy load for only four horses."

"They why didn't you get more horses?"

Longarm bit back an insulting reply and answered, "I forgot."

Alice placed her hand on her shapely hips. "You forgot!"

"Yes, ma'am."

"*Miss* . . . not ma'am . . . you oversized imbecile!"

Big Mamma saved Longarm from a scorching reply to the young woman. "Custis is doing the best he can up here. You've just got to learn some patience."

"I'm learning that this trip wasn't very well planned

50

out," Alice snapped. "If it was planned out at all. Georgia, I thought you were supposed to make sure that this sort of thing didn't happen."

"Kindly address me as Big Mamma."

"You're not my mamma."

Longarm expected to hear an explosion from the woman at his side, but it wasn't forthcoming, so he growled, "We'd better load up and get rolling. We don't want to be caught out here on the road after dark."

"Why not?" Alice demanded.

"Wolves. They've been known to attack the horses and pull the passengers out of coaches."

Alice swallowed, squared her shoulders, and said, "Sir, I don't believe they would be capable of that."

"Suit yourself," Longarm told her. "But I don't care to have a pack of timber wolves attack."

"Nor do I," Big Mamma said. "Load up, Love Sisters!"

Alice told the others about the wolves, and they were loaded and moving up the road in no time at all.

"Have you always been such an accomplished liar?" Big Mamma asked.

"You think I'm accomplished?"

"I certainly do. Even I know that timber wolves can't open stagecoach doors and drag their victims out into the forest to eat."

"That's true, but these ladies are gonna have to start minding us or this mission is doomed." Longarm glanced sideways at the woman. "I'm telling you that there are a lot of men up in these mountains who will do whatever they can to seduce, cheat, rob, or rape these girls."

"You knew that it wasn't going to be an easy job."

"Yeah," Longarm admitted, "I knew. But I didn't realize that they were all going to be so difficult. I don't see how we can handle them. Alice Fairchild alone would damn near be a full-time job."

Georgia O'Grady laughed. She had a deep, throaty

51

laugh that made Longarm feel good, and he had a feeling that he was going to find her irresistible before they were through with this assignment.

"Custis, may I ask you a personal question?"

"You can ask but I might not answer. At least, not truthfully."

"Have you ever been married?"

"No."

"Why not?"

"My line of work don't suit me for marriage."

"And," Big Mamma said, "I don't suppose you'd ever consider changing your profession."

"Why should I?" Longarm leaned forward and slapped the reins against four rumps as they hit an especially steep part of the road. "I'm good at what I do."

"I'm sure that you are. I just thought that you might be good at a lot of things."

"Like what, for instance?"

"You have the size and the build to be an excellent pugilist. I was thinking that you might make a lot more money prizefighting than being a lawman."

Longarm shook his head. "The last thing I'd want to do for a living is toe the mark against a bunch of bruisers intent on knocking me silly."

"I've been studying your hands. You've had some knuckle damage, so don't tell me that you haven't had your share of fistfights."

"It comes with the job."

"Yes, I'm sure that it does. I also notice that your nose hasn't been broken. That tells me you usually win."

"I do," Longarm admitted. "But I don't fight by any ring rules. I hit first and I try to do it with something other than my fists. I've seen men slam an opponent in the jaw with a hell of a punch, but then lose the fight because of a broken hand."

"That happens," Big Mamma agreed. "My husband always taught his students to aim for the solar plexus or the neck just for that reason of saving your hands from injury."

"If you smash a fella in the throat, it swells up and he might die," Longarm said. "That would get you a long prison sentence."

"That's why it's better to go for his groin, his solar plexus, or hit him in the side of the neck or on the beak," Big Mamma explained. "The nose is a cushion, and it usually saves a man's knuckles while taking the fight out of your opponent."

"That makes sense." Longarm frowned. "I've become real good at pistol-whipping someone who is raisin' hell or after my hide. I've learned to tap them on the head just hard enough to put them to sleep. It works especially well with ornery drunks."

They rode along in silence for a while, and Longarm could see that his horses were really starting to blow hard because of the grade, so he pulled them up to catch their breath. "You ladies can get out and take another trip into the trees, if you want."

"What are we stopping for this time? And what about those timber wolves?" Martha asked.

"I'll keep an eye out for them, and so will Big Mamma," Longarm said. He struggled to smother a grin. "And anyway, even if we do lose a couple of you Love Sisters, the rest are enough to do the job."

Martha and the others stared up at him in disbelief. The one named Linda placed her hands on her hips and said, "Miss O'Grady, I think we should replace our driver. He is boorish, insensitive, and a bald-faced liar. He's trying to intimidate us, and I for one will not accept that kind of sadistic behavior!"

"You think I'm sadistic?" Longarm asked, looking down at the bunch of them. "Is that what you think?"

"It sure is!" Cassie cried.

53

"Now, that hurts my poor feelings," Longarm told them. "And it makes me even sadder to have to tell you lovely ladies that, because of us only having four smallish saddle horses and this wagon being so heavy and the road so steep, you are all gonna have to walk the rest of the way up this mountain."

"Never!" Alice Fairchild shouted.

"Sorry," Longarm told her. "But you can tell from looking at these poor animals that they just can't make the grade without us lightening the load. In addition to walking, I'm afraid you'll also need to unload your luggage and carry it to the top."

"Are you out of your mind?" Cassie shouted.

"No, miss, but I am running out of patience. Now get your luggage unloaded and start walking!"

Their eyes locked, and when the Love Sisters stood their ground in defiance, Longarm hopped down from the driver's seat, went around behind the stagecoach, and began to unload the women's baggage, dropping each piece unceremoniously into the dirt.

"Miss O'Grady!" Cassie stormed. "This is absolutely intolerable. You must do something to stop him!"

"I can't," she said. "I'm up here and I've been watching these horses struggle. Custis is right when he says that they won't make it up any farther unless we lighten the load. And that means I'll be walking too."

"But—"

"Look!" Cassie shouted. "A coach is coming down the hill! Perhaps we can pay him to change directions and take us up this awful mountain in style."

Longarm started to object, but Georgia O'Grady whispered, "If Cassie and a few of them quit and return to Denver, it will make things far more manageable."

"Yeah, I see what you mean."

Most of the girls ran out onto the road and when the coach stopped, they pushed up to the door. It swung open, and they recoiled to see that the coach was already full of passengers.

"What do you ladies want?" the gray-bearded driver shouted. "Get back or you'll scare my horses."

"We'd like to know if you'd be willing to turn around and take us back up this awful mountain," Cassie told him.

"What!"

"If we paid you . . . of course."

"Ladies, you're crazy! I got a schedule to keep. Now get outta the road or I'll have to run you down and that'd sure be a waste."

"But wait," Linda shouted, tearing open her purse and waving a handful of money at the driver. "We *can* pay you handsomely . . . girls . . . help me!"

When some of the Love Sisters also began to pull money from their purses, Big Mamma said, "Ladies, I thought we had a mission of mercy to perform up in the mining camps."

"Later," Cassie snapped up at her. "We didn't come clear out here to be treated like draft animals. We want to return to Denver now!"

"If you do that, you're finished with us," Big Mamma warned. "We aren't coming back for anybody."

"That's fine with me," Cassie hissed.

"Miss, gawdammit," the driver swore. "Can't you see that I already got a *full* coach of payin' passengers?"

"I'd be willing to sit on top and let the lady have my seat for . . . ten dollars and . . . and a kiss," a miner quickly offered.

"You got a deal, big boy! Come on out of there right now."

The miner jumped out of the coach, and was followed by two more eager to trade their seats for the same terms. Cassie went right up to the man and gave him a kiss that brought smiles and laughter to the other passengers, except for a middle-aged woman and her husband, who clearly thought the behavior was scandalous.

"Me next," a dirty miner with bad teeth said, throwing himself out of the coach and landing in the dirt a moment before scrambling back to his feet.

"Mister," Linda told him, "I'll give you twenty dollars, but I'll be darned if you'll kiss my lips."

The miner's smile died, but he held out his hand. "Twenty dollars and it's less than twenty miles down to Denver in good weather. Hell, I'll take that any time."

Linda paid the man, and Martha, the fragile girl with red hair, told the last miner, "I'll give you two kisses and no money."

"I'll take that offer," the miner said, scooping her up in his arms, bending her over so far that Longarm thought her back might snap, and kissing her passionately while the other men whooped with appreciation and loaded their baggage.

"Golly," Martha breathed, looking a little dizzy. "That was really a good kiss!"

"You want more, little lady?"

"I better not," Martha said, wobbling up to the coach and accepting help climbing inside.

The bearded driver looked at Big Mamma and said, "I'd give you ten dollars and a ride, lady."

"No, thanks."

The driver looked hopefully at Elizabeth, Milly and Alice Fairchild. "You girls aren't quite as attractive as the big one, but I'd give you a free ride up here with me for a little tickle or two."

"Get lost, you old reprobate!" Elizabeth snapped. "I wouldn't let you touch me with a ten-foot pole."

"Well that suits me just fine too then!" the driver said, highly insulted. "Is everyone ready to roll?"

When the word came back that everyone was ready, the driver tipped his hat to Big Mamma and said, "How about twenty dollars and we play a little patty-cake up here on the driver's seat?"

Georgia laughed. "No, thanks. Besides, I'd probably end up busting your jaw long before we reached the city limits of Denver."

"And miss, you look like you'd be woman enough to do it! So long!"

Longarm waved and was feeling better. Three down, he thought, and three to go. Four if I count Big Mamma, but I'm enjoying her company so she don't count.

"Now that we're lighter, can we all get back into the coach?" Alice wanted to know.

"I guess," Longarm told her.

"If you expect me to thank you for changing your mind, you're in for a big disappointment."

"Miss Fairchild," Longarm drawled, "I doubt if you are in the habit of thanking anyone . . . even your grandfather, the President."

"I don't like our driver," Alice said to Big Mamma. "And I want him replaced at the earliest opportunity."

"He stays," Georgia replied. "And I'm surprised that you chose not to quit like those other three."

"I'm not a quitter," Alice snapped as she grabbed her own luggage and hurled it into the coach before climbing in herself. "But I'm not going to be taken advantage of either."

It was almost dark when they finally struggled up to the modest little boardinghouse where they'd spend the night.

Longarm pulled up in front of the place and shouted, "Everyone out!"

The Love Sisters were not feeling very loving. In fact, they were rumpled and cranky. Alice said something nasty to Elizabeth, who snapped back a quick insult that was quite unladylike. Even Milly, the dark-haired and angelic-looking one who rarely spoke, looked irritable, and stomped into the boardinghouse without waiting for anyone.

"I better go inside and talk to the owner," Longarm said, easing down from the driver's seat and grunting with pain.

"What's the matter with your backside?"

"Nothing."

"Oh, really? Then explain why you have a bloodstain on the seat of your pants."

"I'd rather not discuss it."

"That's no boil on your butt."

"Never mind," Longarm growled.

Big Mamma grabbed him. "Let's not be prissy about something that is important. Custis, you need medical attention."

"Look," he said, shaking her off. "I can bandage myself."

"Are you embarrassed by this?"

Longarm was glad that the light was poor because he was sure that he was blushing. He started to lie, then changed his mind. "Okay, Georgia, I *am* embarrassed."

"What is the nature of this wound?"

"I was shot in the buttocks just before you arrived." Longarm had no intention of explaining the circumstances behind getting shot. "It burns like fire and I can't keep a bandage on my butt."

"Small wonder," Big Mamma said with a straight face. "After everything has settled down and we can find a way to be alone, I'll clean it up, put a bandage on the wound, and wash the bloodstains from your pants."

"I appreciate your offer, but no, thanks."

Big Mamma put her hands on her hips and looked him right in the eye. "Mister, it could get infected and then where'd you be?"

Longarm knew the woman was right. But how humiliating!

Big Mamma chuckled. "Don't worry, Marshal. This will remain our little secret. Did you pack a clean pair of pants?"

"Sure."

"Good. I know how to fix cuts, although I admit that I've never patched up *that* part of a man's anatomy. I've got something to promote the healing, but it stings at first."

"I don't care."

"All right then," Georgia said. "Let's go inside and see if we can get the Love Sisters bedded down for the night."

Longarm gritted his teeth and followed Big Mamma into the rooming house. He'd never been inside the place before, but it had been recommended, and now as he entered the house, he could see why. The parlor was spotless and tastefully decorated. The small, gray-haired woman who formally greeted them was dressed as if she were going to church.

"I've only three rooms unoccupied," the older woman told them after introducing herself as Mrs. Huntington. "But each room has two beds and a bathtub, which we will fill with hot water at no additional cost. So, if the four ladies will take two rooms, sir, you can take the third."

"That will be just fine."

"Where are the three young ladies?" Georgia asked.

"They paid and hurried off to their rooms," the woman replied. She frowned and wrung her hands. "They are lovely young ladies, but I did not find them especially very talkative."

"They've come a long way and are extremely weary," Big Mamma explained. "We are all exhausted and wish to take our baths and go to bed early."

"Would you like to dine before retiring?" Mrs. Huntington asked.

"I think not," Big Mamma told their hostess. "But I'm quite sure that Mr. Long is famished."

"I am," he admitted. "But before I fill my own belly, I've got to unhitch, feed, and water the team."

"You will find the barn around on the other side of the house," Mrs. Huntington said. "There are corrals and a stack of good grass hay. I charge my guests two bits per animal, which I believe to be a reasonable price."

"It is," Longarm agreed. "Those horses pulled that big coach and us up from Denver and I'd like to grain them heavy."

The woman smiled. "You will find sacks of barley and oats in the barn. Help yourself and we'll add just one more dollar. That's what I charge for each guest."

Longarm started to ask the woman if she would accept a government voucher, but he changed his mind, knowing that she would not. Besides, Billy Vail had given him two hundred dollars in cash so that he could pay most if not all of his expenses. As for the women . . . well, Longarm had a feeling they could go through a lot of money fast.

He reached for his wallet as Big Mamma said, "The Love Sisters will pay our own expenses. I'm sorry we cannot also pay for yours."

"Not a problem," he told her.

They paid Mrs. Huntington, who said, "It won't take long to prepare your supper, sir. Would steak and potatoes with cooked carrots be all right?"

"Perfect," Longarm said, heading outside to take care of his horses. Later, when he returned to the boarding-house, he enjoyed a fine supper.

"Do you mind if I ask you a rather personal question?" Mrs. Huntington asked, sitting down at the table to rest for a moment.

"I suppose not."

Mrs. Huntington fidgeted for a moment or two, then blurted out, "Why are you bleeding from the behind? That must hurt something awful and you should see a doctor at once."

"You noticed, huh?"

"Oh, yes! I am worried about you."

"Don't be. I'll be fine."

But Mrs. Huntington wasn't listening. "My late husband died of cancer and had exactly that kind of bleeding from the . . . the backside. I fear you might have the same affliction."

Longarm raised his head and finished chewing. "Ma'am," he said, seeing that the woman really was upset, "the truth of the matter is that I had a little accident. The bleeding is *not* from a cancer, but from a flesh wound."

"Oh, thank heavens!" Mrs. Huntington jumped up and scurried into her kitchen. "I have water heating on the stove. It's ready for the baths."

"Are you going to haul it to the rooms yourself?"

"Oh, no! I have a Chinaman and his wife who live out back. Mrs. Chang will help me."

"Good," Longarm said, thinking that the woman didn't look strong enough to be lugging buckets of hot bathwater back and forth from the kitchen to the rooms.

He finished his meal, then went to his room. Mr. Chang soon appeared with hot water, and Longarm wasted no time easing into the tub. The hot water really burned his buttocks at first. Then they began to feel better.

Longarm lay soaking his behind in the tub for quite some time. He might even have dozed off because, the next thing he knew, Big Mamma was soaping up a washrag and shampooing his hair.

"I don't know about this," he said, loving it. "We hardly know each other and here you are treating me like we were—"

"What? Man and wife?"

"No. Lovers."

"I'm going to give you a shave and scrub you up good,"

61

Big Mamma said. "Then we'll doctor that wound, let it dry, and put a good bandage on it that you will find much more useful and comfortable."

Longarm smiled with contentment. "There's a cigar and a bottle of whiskey over on the bedside table. Do you mind if I smoke and have a drink?"

"Not as long as I can join you."

"You smoke?"

"I enjoy a cigar on occasion, and a good glass of whiskey is always a joy."

His eyelids were heavy, but he opened them and looked up at Georgia O'Grady. Her face was damp with perspiration and she wasn't as pretty as the other Love Sisters, but she was definitely his favorite. "Then let's smoke and have a drink together."

"I'd like that after I wash the dirt from behind your ears and doctor your behind."

Longarm chuckled. "Georgia, you tell me you can whip and outshoot most men and I have no reason to doubt that claim. You can doctor a wound and you like to smoke and drink. Is there anything you *can't* or *won't* do?"

"Yes," she said sweetly, "I won't become your lover."

He blinked. "Why not?"

"Because we both have important jobs to do. If we started cooing and screwing, we'd start messing everything up in a hurry."

"Not necessarily."

"Oh, yes, we would." Georgia reached down into the water and grabbed Longarm's flaccid tool. "Big Boy, you just keep this long and soft and everything will stay just fine between us. Understood?"

Before Longarm could form an answer, her strong hand slipped lower and cupped his sack. She squeezed just hard enough that he sat up straight, nodded his head vigorously, and choked, "Whatever you say, Big Mamma!"

"Good. Now climb out of there and let's see what we have to work on tonight."

Longarm meekly obeyed the woman. He was not in any position to challenge her authority tonight. However, before this assignment was finished, he had a hunch that things might dramatically change for the better.

Chapter 6

Longarm awakened early the next morning and gently patted his behind. The bandage that Big Mamma had applied the night before was still in place and the wound felt better. Pleased, he shaved, dressed in clean clothes, and tiptoed into the dining room, where Mrs. Huntington surprised him by not only being awake, but having a fresh pot of coffee ready for her guests.

"Good morning, ma'am."

"Good morning. Sit down and let me pour you a cup of coffee."

"Thanks. I drink it black."

The woman smiled. "My late husband took it straight too. I prefer cream and sugar, which seems to make it easier on the stomach."

"Yes, ma'am." Longarm stifled a yawn and gazed around the room. "You have a nice boardinghouse."

"A widow has to find some way to make a living. And I enjoy the guests . . . most of the time. I get a strange one now and then. But I'm pretty careful who I let stay the night. If I see signs of lice or too much liquor, I'll turn a person away no matter how hard they plead."

Mrs. Huntington dropped another sugar cube into her

coffee and stirred it thoughtfully. "I do get quite a few characters dropping in, but I've never really felt my life was in any real danger."

"That's good."

"And," she added slyly, "I keep a loaded derringer in the cookie jar, just in case."

"Not a bad idea, ma'am."

"So who are you and what are you doing with these lovely ladies?"

"I'm just a driver and they are a traveling group of singers."

"Really?" Mrs. Huntington pinned him with her eyes.

"Yes. Or so I've been told."

"You mean you haven't even heard them sing?"

"No. I picked them up in Denver and they wanted to do a tour of some of the mining camps. I just drive and keep to my own business, Mrs. Huntington."

"Like I should. Right?"

"I didn't say that."

"Yes, you did. But in such a nice way that it's all right." The old lady sipped her coffee and peered over her cup at Longarm. "Is it too strong?"

"Just right."

"Good. Forgive me for asking, but how is your backside this fine morning?"

"Much better."

"I'm glad you told me it was just a flesh wound and not a stomach cancer. I was wondering about that great big woman. She seems in charge."

"She is."

Mrs. Huntington frowned. "I've seen traveling shows come through here many a time, but I never saw one that had so much money. They must be very good."

Longarm knew that the woman was trying to worm information out of him, but he was determined to tell her nothing. If Big Mamma wanted to tell the truth, that was fine coming from her lips, but not his.

"Are all those young ladies from back East?"

"That's right."

"Why would such refined and lovely girls ever want to come to this rough, dirty mining country?"

Before Longarm could form a reply, the woman continued. "Oh, I'm not saying it isn't beautiful up here. I've been back East, and I wouldn't trade all of it for the Colorado Rockies, but still, it is rough and rugged. Those girls looked very upset last night."

"They were really tired." Longarm drained his cup, and it was instantly refilled to the brim.

"Sir, you strike me as a man who is more than a stage driver."

"Oh?"

"Yes. You strike me as a man of . . . of *authority*."

He chuckled. "Mrs. Huntington, I have authority over four horses, but not much of anything else."

"So you say," she said demurely. "But I think that there is something afoot here that is much more interesting than a mere choral group traveling about trying to entertain and gain profit."

Longarm considered his coffee as if the brew held important answers to important questions.

Mrs. Huntington cleared her throat loudly. "You must forgive me, but I'm rather forgetful. Did you say where you were going today?"

"Up to Gold Creek."

"That's not so far. I might ride along with your girls just to see them perform . . . if that is agreeable."

"It is with me, but you'll have to ask Big Mamma."

Mrs. Huntington made a face as if she'd bitten into a sour pickle. "Such an unladylike name! Surely she has a *real* and much prettier-sounding one."

"Her real name is Mrs. Georgia O'Grady."

"Oh, then she's a *married* woman."

"No," Longarm explained. "Her husband was a prize-fighter, but he was poisoned and killed."

The old lady shivered with excitement. "How very interesting!"

Longarm picked up his coffee and stood ready to leave. "I'm going to take this cup out to the corral and check on my horses. I'll bring it back."

"Then I'll refill it as often as you like. I drink coffee all day long and it makes me a little silly at times, but I love the taste."

Longarm smiled and strolled out to the corral. He pitched more grass hay to the animals, and fed them another heavy ration of grain. They looked much better this morning, just as he supposed that he did.

"Good morning," a small but cheerful voice said in greeting.

Longarm pivoted about to see the black-haired angelic one named Milly. "Good morning," he replied. "You're up early."

"And so are you." Milly came over to join him by the horses. "They had a hard time yesterday."

"I'm afraid our stagecoach is too heavy and the grade was steep."

"Will it be as difficult today?"

Longarm set his pitchfork down and shook his head. "No. Gold Creek is only about ten more miles. We should be there this afternoon."

"And then what?"

"I have no idea," he said honestly. "I would expect that Mrs. O'Grady and you ladies would have some kind of a plan."

Milly shrugged her shoulders and spread her palms upright, reminding Longarm of a little pixie. "I'm afraid we don't have any kind of plan."

"Well," Longarm told her, "you had better come up

with one because you ladies are going to cause quite a stir wherever you go."

"I suppose." Milly leaned between the rails to watch the horses eat. She was a lovely young woman and quite full-bodied, now that he had a chance to really study her closely.

She turned and caught him staring, then blushed and said, "Do you find my posterior as interesting as we ladies found yours yesterday?"

It was Longarm's turn to blush. "I'm sorry."

"Don't be," Milly told him, straightening and coming a step closer. "I like to be admired. Were you admiring me?"

"I sure was."

"And at such an early hour!" Milly giggled. "That makes it an even greater compliment."

"I'm glad that you aren't offended."

"Oh, no!" The young woman smiled. "Listen, I come from a large family and I have three older brothers. I know what boys think and talk about."

"You do?"

"Of course! They talk about girls." She looked him up and down. "But you're not a boy, so I suppose you think and talk about women."

"Not really."

She frowned. "I can't believe that."

"It's the truth. I love women. I find them endlessly fascinating, but also a complete mystery. And since I don't understand them, I don't waste time thinking or talking about them all that much." Longarm leaned back against the pole corral. "Does that make any sense to you?"

"In a roundabout way it does. But you really don't talk about women?"

"No. You see, I was raised in the South and taught that a man does not discuss women. He can admire . . . even

68

cherish them . . . but he does not talk about them, especially about anything that might soil their reputations as ladies."

"I see. You don't look much like the gentlemen I know, but I suppose that looks can be very deceiving."

Longarm didn't know where this conversation was leading, but he had a hunch Milly did. "Deceiving, huh?"

"Oh, yes," she said with great certainty. "Take my looks, for example."

"All right. You are a lovely lady."

"I know. I've been told that often enough that it's easy to believe. But I've also been told that I possess a pious or reverential quality. Would you agree?"

"I . . . I don't know." Longarm was off balance and trying hard to figure this woman out. "You look quite innocent, if that is what you mean."

"That's exactly what I mean. Now, those three girls that quit the Love Sisters, did any of them look innocent?"

Though the morning was brisk, Longarm felt a flush of perspiration. "Miss, you're asking me a question I'd prefer not to answer."

"Because of your Southern breeding. Well, if you were honest and candid, you would say that none of those three looked innocent."

"All right."

"But I do look innocent. Like a little choir girl."

"You do."

"Well, I'm not."

Longarm's jaw sagged. "Miss?"

Milly's delicate chin lifted with a touch of newfound defiance. "The honest truth is that I *love* making love to men. And I came West not only to help the poor women in mining camps, but to choose a few men and make love to them whenever and wherever I could at every opportunity."

"I . . . I see."

Milly reached out and took his hand. "And right now, I want to make love in that pile of hay with *you*."

"Now wait a minute!"

"It's a most beautiful morning. You have bathed and I see you in a completely different light than I did yesterday. You're a former Southern gentleman and now a true man of the West. So how about it?"

Longarm swallowed. "Dammit, Milly, I'm supposed to be *guarding* you."

"Of course you are!" Milly took his other hand and pressed it to her bosom. "Do you really believe that we thought you were just a stagecoach driver? Good heavens! I'll bet you are a lawman, and a very special one to be picked to protect the President's granddaughter. And I have another feeling about you."

"Spit it out."

"I don't think you got a splinter in your butt. I think you were probably shot flying out of some married woman's bedroom." Milly slipped her arms around his waist and stared intently up into his eyes. "Am I wrong?"

"You got the main part of it right," he admitted.

"Then why don't we . . . how do you say it? Mosey! That's what you people say! Why don't we mosey over to that big stack of grass hay and have a wonderful time together."

"Listen, Milly, I—"

She raised up on her tiptoes and kissed his mouth hard. Then she whispered, "Time is wasting and I'm just dying to have a *real* cowboy."

"I'm not a cowboy."

"Of course not. You're something even more exciting. Let's do it!"

Longarm could scarcely believe what he was hearing. But he could hear the blood starting to pound in his ears and he felt something else starting to throb, so he glanced back at the house to make sure that Mrs. Huntington wasn't watching, and then he nodded in agreement.

It took them less than two minutes to undress and leap into the stack of sweet-smelling grass hay. It took less than two minutes more of kissing and exploring before Milly guided his big, stiff rod into her hungry womanhood. Milly wrapped her girlish legs around his waist and giggled.

"What's so funny!"

"I've been wondering what kind of a place I'd first get laid in in the West, and what kind of a man I'd be with, and this beats anything I dreamed."

Longarm's hips moved powerfully, and Milly surprised him with her own strength and smooth hip action. "Welcome to the Wild West," he grunted.

"Ride me like you were a big stallion and I was your prettiest, most favorite filly."

"My pleasure," he panted, surging powerfully in and out of her slick honey pot.

"Mine too."

Milly clung to him. She was such a little thing that he was almost afraid to really get vigorous, but Milly let him know by touch and her moaning that she wanted all he could give her and then some.

"Say something Western to me," she pleaded, squeezing her black eyes shut. "Say something wild and Western!"

"Yahoo!" he shouted, thrusting harder and harder until Milly began to shiver and then lose control of her lovely little body. "Yahoo!"

"Ride me, cowboy!" she pleaded, raking his back with her perfect little fingernails.

Longarm burst like a dam and drove his torrent deep into her body. She was like a thrashing wildcat and kept yelling, "Ride me, cowboy!"

And all he could think of was to shout, "Yahoo!"

• • •

"Here," she said, looking a little dazed after they dressed, "let me pick the hay off the back of your pants and shirt."

"I'll do the same for you. If Big Mamma figures out that I did this to you, I'll—"

"I'll tell her it was entirely my idea. That you, being a wild man of the West and a former Southern gentleman, had no choice but to accommodate my animal yearnings."

"I don't think that would help much. I'm supposed to be protecting . . . not screwing the Love Sisters."

"You can just do both." Milly smiled. "Alice is aching for it, and so is that smart-aleck Elizabeth. So just bide your time and give it to them just like you gave it to me. Only, save some so that we can do it again later."

"I don't believe I'm hearing this from a wealthy young lady."

"We're all a lot more women than we are society girls."

Longarm turned her around and picked the last wisps of hay from her hair and clothes. "I think we're presentable again."

"I hope so," Milly said. "Did you slip your long salami to Big Mamma last night?"

"Hell, no!" he snapped, feeling strangely indignant.

"You should do it at the earliest opportunity," Milly advised him with great sincerity. "That way, when she catches us, she can't be such a high-and-mighty hypocrite."

Longarm almost laughed. "I'll keep that very much in mind."

Milly giggled again.

"What's so funny?" he asked.

"I just had an image of you and Big Mamma doing it together in a fit of passion. And it seems to me that mounting that Amazon woman would be akin to riding an African elephant."

Longarm burst out laughing. "That's terrible!"

Milly was nearly in hysterics. "Well, wouldn't it be?"

"No."

"Sure it would, and you'd better be careful or you'll have more than a butt ache!"

Longarm bent over double, laughing and whooping. He hadn't laughed so hard in weeks, and it took them both a good long while to regain their composure.

"We'd better go back inside," Longarm said.

"I'll go in first and try to sneak back to my room without that prying old lady seeing me."

"Good luck."

Milly gave Longarm a farewell kiss, then hurried off, leaving him to realize that you really could never make the mistake of judging someone by their appearances.

Chapter 7

Later, Longarm went to the kitchen, and was surprised to find it empty. But he heard a terrible caterwauling outside, so he poured himself a cup of coffee and proceeded to the porch.

"Oh, no," he groaned when he saw Big Mamma rehearsing the Love Sisters as they tried to sing a popular mining camp ballad called "Grandma's Tears Ran Dry." The song was a real gut-twister, all about a young lady who was lamenting the fact that her grandfather had died of a broken neck after getting drunk and toppling off his faithful mule. Custis had heard the song sung in many a mining camp tent and saloon, and he had to admit it was the kind that would start the hardest miner to weeping. The first few lines went like this:

> When Grandma found Grandpa, he was still
>   alive, it's true,
> but his neck was busted six ways, and his
>   face was mighty blue.
> Well, he told her that he loved her, and he
>   was sorry for drinkin' so much rye,
> but Grandma wasn't cryin' 'cause her tears
>   had all run dry.

If sung well, the ballad was a winner. But when it was done without any voice or talent . . . the way the Love Sisters were doing it now . . . the song seemed . . . well, almost funny. And so, as Big Mamma and the Love Sisters tried to carry a tune, Longarm's initial shocked expression was transformed into a smile, and it was all that he could do not to bust out laughing.

"Girls!" Big Mamma finally wailed with exasperation when the song was finished. "Can't *any* of you sing?"

The Love Sisters were clearly unhappy, and they appeared to already be getting short on patience. Miss Alice snapped, "We don't like that stupid song anyway. Why can't we do some Eastern ones that we know and like?"

"Because you aren't in the East and anyway, what would it matter? You girls sound terrible."

"You can't sing either," Elizabeth said accusingly. "And anyway, why do we need to entertain the miners?"

"You know the reasons," Big Mamma replied. "If they realized that you were all from wealthy families, you'd never have a minute's worth of peace and we surely wouldn't be able to help the mining women."

"Why don't we try dancing?" Milly suggested, offering Longarm a seductive smile.

"Yes," Elizabeth agreed. "Let's try dancing."

But Big Mamma shook her head. "Dancing would incite passion among the miners, and that is the last thing we need from these rough men. Singing sad songs and ballads would remind them of their home and families and keep them on their best behavior. Isn't that right, Custis?"

"I expect so."

"Let's try another song."

"Why?" Alice wanted to know. "If we can't sing, then we can't sing. I say that we drop all this sham of trying to pretend we are a traveling troupe of entertainers and do something else instead."

"Like what?" Big Mamma demanded.

"Why don't we say that we are of some kind of religious order?"

"You mean like *nuns*?" Milly asked, looking appalled.

"Sure!"

"No," Milly said, emphatically shaking her head. "My family is Catholic and I wouldn't think of insulting the Church."

"Fine," Alice said with asperity. "Then we aren't nuns, but we can still be a religious order. Let's just say that we Love Sisters have devoted ourselves to doing charitable acts like helping people out."

"That's a good idea," Mrs. Huntington agreed, coming through the doorway. "Because you sure aren't going to fool anybody with vaudeville or pretending to be a choral group."

"I agree," Longarm said. "Why not just say that you are a religious order and have taken vows of poverty, charity, and chastity."

"Chastity?" Milly repeated. "That means *no men*."

"That's right," Longarm said, managing to maintain a serious expression. "The mountains are filled with rough miners. If they understand that you are committed to chastity and acts of mercy, they'll be respectful. And don't say that you have money to offer needy women. Just act damned good and pious!"

Longarm turned to Big Mamma. "I don't see that you have any choice, given the way these girls sing. And I agree that dancing would incite passion. The men in these mountains are starved for women."

"I don't know," she hedged. "Before coming out from the East, we talked a great deal about what we were to say and how to act in order to do our work and not create problems. It was thought that—"

"Georgia," Longarm interrupted, "it doesn't matter what was thought back East. I'm telling you that the best thing is to keep things simple and admit that the Love

Sisters are here to help women. What you don't have to say is that you are all wealthy and have money to hand out."

"He's right," Alice declared. "And not trying to come up with a stage show performance will make things so much more simple."

"I agree," Milly said.

"Me too," Elizabeth added. "If Cassie and Martha were still here, maybe we could pull this singing thing off because they both had good voices. But Alice and Milly can't carry a tune in a bucket, and I don't want to have to do it all."

"What!" Alice cried with outrage. "I can sing better than you!"

"You sound like a bullfrog," Elizabeth shot back.

"Love Sisters!" Big Mamma shouted. "Let's not squabble!"

Longarm nodded in agreement. "I'll be hitching up the team, ladies. We ought to be pulling out in about an hour."

"Would you like some help?" Elizabeth asked much too eagerly.

"No," Milly snapped in a fit of obvious jealousy, "I'm sure that he wouldn't."

Elizabeth sweetly replied, "Well, my goodness, Milly. You mean you *weren't* out pitching hay to our poor horses with Custis this morning?"

Milly blushed deeply. Big Mamma shot Longarm a look that would kill, and he suddenly decided he needed another cup of coffee.

Early that afternoon when their stagecoach jolted up the potholed streets of Gold Creek, the miners and store owners came rushing out to greet the Love Sisters. It was all that Longarm and Big Mamma could do to try and keep them from actually pulling the three frightened young

77

women out of the coach and having a good time with them right in the street.

"Hold on!" Longarm shouted, setting the stagecoach's brake and jumping to his feet with his gun in his fist. "These are *ladies*."

"They're women," someone shouted. "And we sure need some new women in Gold Creek. So sit down and tell them gals to come out and show us their pretty faces."

Before Longarm could respond, Big Mamma stood up and levered a shell into her rifle. In a deep and menacing voice, she bellowed, "Anyone touches those ladies is gonna take a shortcut to the Promised Land!"

The miners stared up at her and then retreated a few paces. "Are you man . . . or woman?" one small, ferret-faced miner asked, squinting upward.

"I'm in charge of protecting those ladies. And for your information, we are very religious."

"They nuns?" a tall, curly-haired man asked.

"Not exactly," Big Mamma hedged.

"What exactly do you mean by that, ma'am?"

"I mean that they are sort of like nuns. They have sworn themselves to charity and chastity and call themselves the Love Sisters."

"Well any one of 'em can start by lovin' me!" a toady little fella with a bottle of whiskey in his hand howled gleefully, spreading his arms and legs out wide as the others cheered and shouted similar enthusiastic offers.

Right about then, Longarm figured that he might just need to yank out his United States marshal's badge and establish his authority. But just when he was reaching for his badge, Miss Alice Fairchild, granddaughter of the President, threw open the door and stood on the first step of the coach with an expression on her face that would chill the passion of any man.

"Just who do you people think you are to act this way in our presence!" she demanded, her eyes raking the crude assembly. "We've come here to help your women find a better life in these miserable, godforsaken camps. You are acting like a bunch of hooligans and ignorant boors. How dare you behave in this manner! Are there no gentlemen among the entire lot of you? Not one man who was taught by a priest or a minister that women are to be cherished and protected? Have not one of you had a dear and loving mother that taught you any proper manners?"

Longarm couldn't see Alice Fairchild's face, but he could feel her righteous indignation and well imagine her fierce expression because he saw the impact she had on the crowd. One minute they were riotous and bawdy, the next shamed by her scathing tirade.

"I . . . I'm sorry, miss," the one with the bottle said, barely able to raise his face to Alice. "I do have a dear, loving mother and she did teach me better. Will you forgive my bad manners?"

The crowd held its shamed silence until Alice, her voice softening, replied, "Yes, I do forgive you. Now, would you all please go back about your business so that we can find food and lodging?"

The crowd backed away in respectful silence, and Longarm just had to shake his head in wonder as he released the hand brake and sent the coach on down the street to a boardinghouse that he hoped would take in these four women.

"Can you believe that?" Big Mamma asked in obvious amazement. "I knew that Alice Fairchild had a temper, but I never realized she could use it so effectively. Why, she really scorched their pride."

"That she did," Longarm agreed. "I saw some steel in that young lady that I hadn't realized she possessed."

"Me neither." Big Mamma looked aside at him. "So what *did* happen out in the hay pile with our sweet Milly this morning?"

"Better you don't ask."

"Yeah, I guess not. But I am disappointed in you, Custis. I remember you promised to protect the Love Sisters."

"I did and I will."

"And you call humping Milly protecting her?" Big Mamma's voice had taken on a hard, accusing edge. "Is that what you call it?"

"Look," he replied. "I didn't go after the girl. I didn't even want it to happen. But it just did and I don't want to talk about it. Understand?"

"I understand," Big Mamma grated with anger in her voice. "And since you've broken your promise to be a gentleman, I'm going to have to find someone else that I can trust with the Love Sisters."

Longarm's head swung toward the woman. "Georgia, what are you saying?"

"I'm saying you are fired, Marshal Long. I'm going to wire your superiors in Denver and demand that they send us someone with morals and integrity."

Longarm knew that he had broken his promise and deserved to be dressed down. What he also knew was that he had formed an attachment to the Love Sisters and especially Big Mamma. "I'm sorry about what happened. I'll try not to do it again."

"I don't believe you."

"I'm a man, dammit! Milly came and practically jumped me. I was surprised and by the time I got to thinking, we were—"

"Oh, spare me!" Big Mamma told him. "I misjudged you quite badly. So when we are properly lodged here in Gold Creek, just . . . just return to Denver."

Longarm expelled a deep breath. "I can't do that, Georgia."

"Of course you can!"

"No, I can't," he said very deliberately. "Because if I do and something really terrible happens to you or one of the other Love Sisters, I'll always hold myself to blame."

"After what you've just admitted, are you trying to convince me that you have a conscience?"

Longarm considered his response carefully. "Yes, I am. I didn't do anything that Milly hasn't already done before many times. She needed a man and I needed a woman. It was good for both of us and did no harm."

"Oh, really?" Big Mamma raised her eyebrows in a question. "Well, don't you think that now that Milly has . . . enjoyed you . . . that Alice and Elizabeth will find you similarly irresistible? That they'll also want to sample what you have to offer?"

"I hadn't thought of that."

"Well, I have."

Longarm pulled the coach up in front of the boarding-house he had in mind. "The couple that own this are a Baptist minister and his wife. They only take in ladies and they are good, kind Christian people. You'll all do fine here."

"Unless they catch you humping one of my girls."

"Georgia, I'll say one more time that I am sorry. And for what it's worth, I am not in the habit of apologizing to anyone. I did promise not to fool around with any of your girls and I failed my word."

She looked him right in the eye. "Does that mean you swear on the holy Bible that you won't 'fail' again?"

"I . . . I can't quite do that," he was forced to admit as the image of Milly's luscious, bare, and hungry body flashed before his eyes.

"Then I stand by what I said before," Georgia told him, eyes misting with tears. "You are fired and I will telegraph Denver and ask for your replacement."

"Georgia, you can't do that."

"Oh, really? You'll see!"

"I mean, you can't do that because there isn't a telegraph line that comes this far up the mountain."

Caught off guard, the woman quickly recovered to de-

81

clare, "Then by heavens I will write your Director a letter!"

"You can do that all right," Longarm admitted. "But I wish you would calm down for a day or two and reconsider. There's not a man more suited for this job than myself. I know that I've let you down, but if trouble comes, and I mean bad trouble . . . you won't find anyone better to have on your side."

"That remark smacks of arrogance. It is just man talk like I've heard from so many of the prizefighters before they toed the mark with my late husband and then had their heads practically handed to them."

"I can back up my talk like Shamus," he vowed. "If I couldn't, Director Cardiff and my immediate superior, Billy Vail, would never have asked me to take this job. And, for your information, I tried to turn them down."

"I wish they'd have accepted your refusal."

"Not me. Because, if they'd have found someone else, we wouldn't have gotten to know each other and become friends."

In reply, Big Mamma twisted around and threw a short, powerful uppercut to Longarm's ribs that doubled him up in pain.

"Satisfied now?" he wheezed.

"Yes."

"Does that mean that you're giving me the chance to finish this assignment?"

"Are you going to also do it to Alice and Elizabeth when my back is turned some night?"

"I'll do my best not to."

"Hmmph!" she snorted. "And if I believe that, I'm a damned dumb fool!"

Longarm managed a smile. "Thanks, and I'd appreciate it if you'd rebandage my butt tonight," he said as he eased down from the driver's seat, ducking a swift overhand right aimed for his square jaw.

• • •

The Reverend Paul Porter had been preaching and saving souls since he was eighteen years old, and his wife, Esther, was sweet and God-fearing. "Welcome," they both said with an enthusiastic greeting. "Welcome to our humble home!"

Longarm stepped aside as Big Mamma explained the reason for their visit, and ended up by saying, "We are just looking to spread a little charity on the women of these mining towns and need safe lodging."

"You will have it here," the reverend promised. He looked over at Longarm. "And what about you, sir?"

"I'll find accommodations in town."

"Very good."

Longarm stayed for a few moments while the good reverend and his wife showed the Love Sisters their rooms. After that, he climbed back onto the stagecoach and drove it up the street to the only livery in Gold Creek.

"Howdy," a huge, middle-aged man with shaggy brown hair and bib overalls said in greeting. "Do you need a place to put up them horses?"

"I sure do."

"You're the one that drove them Love Sisters in, aren't you?"

"That's right."

"Well, maybe you could introduce me to that big gal that was up top riding shotgun for you. She sure was a looker!"

"She is that."

"She married?"

"Widowed."

The liveryman grinned, revealing that his front upper and lower teeth were missing. "That's real good news! Tell you what. You introduce me to that mountain of womanhood and I'll let you board this team for a dollar a day. That's half the going rate."

"No, thanks."

The man's face fell. "Why not?"

"I'm just the driver and I've fallen out of favor with that lady. Besides, she is here to do charity, not find a husband."

"Could be she can handle both."

Longarm's butt was aching, but at least he wasn't bleeding from the embarrassing wound anymore. "Where can a man find a good room and some hot food?"

"Try the Lone Bear Lodge. I heard they got ticks in the bedding, but no lice, and the rooms are reasonable. As for food, there's a little cafe next door to the lodge that serves good stew and chili."

"I'm in the mood for a steak dinner."

"Then you better try someplace else." The liveryman frowned. "Are you sure you can't give me a little introduction to that big woman with the big udders?"

"The what?"

"You know. Teats."

"Nope."

"Then the four horses will cost you two dollars a day. Cash in advance."

Longarm paid the man and went to get a steak and a room. He didn't spend much time in the gambling halls or saloons that night, but what time he did spend was taken up with trying to fend off offers similar to the one he'd received at the livery stable.

"Those are righteous women," he kept saying. "They are ladies."

"Ladies was just meant to be turned into wild women," one half-soused miner bragged. "And I'm just the man to do it!"

There was no doubt that the Love Sisters had made a huge impression on the little mining community. They were all that anyone wanted to discuss, and when Longarm grew weary of trying to explain that they were very religious and not interested in going to bed with men, the miners snickered and wanted to argue the fact. After a while, Longarm was fed up with the talk and went to bed.

When he awoke in the morning, the sun was shining through his bedroom window. Longarm yawned, turned over, and decided he'd go back to sleep for a while. He was just starting to drift off when he was jolted erect by a loud pounding on his door.

"Go away!"

There was a tremendous crash and splintering of wood a moment before Big Mamma appeared, looking pale and excited. "You gotta help me!"

"What's wrong?"

"Milly is gone!"

Longarm blinked. "What do you mean 'gone'?"

"She's missing, dammit!"

Longarm was wearing his flannel underwear, and now he grabbed for his shirt, boots, and pants. "Any idea what happened?"

"Someone came through her bedroom window last night and grabbed the poor girl," Big Mamma answered.

"Georgia, she's not an innocent virgin. It could be that she sneaked out looking for some excitement."

"Custis, there's bloodstains on Milly's bedsheets, and even more on her windowsill, so I know she didn't go willingly."

Longarm jumped into his pants and quickly finished dressing. He strapped on his gunbelt and followed Big Mamma out the door.

"Custis, if someone raped and killed that little girl, there is just going to be hell to pay!"

"I know. Don't worry, we'll find her."

"I believe you," Big Mamma said, "but I wonder if we'll find her dead or alive."

Georgia O'Grady was hoping for a positive answer. One that would ease her mind. But Longarm wasn't going to raise any false hopes, because any man bold enough to abduct a young lady through her bedroom window was the kind that just might decide to kill her after he'd had his pleasure.

Chapter 8

By the time Longarm and Big Mamma reached the Porter residence, the entire household was in an uproar. Longarm barged through the front door and took in the chaotic scene at a glance.

"Which room was Milly sleeping in?"

"The one right down the hallway next to mine," Alice Fairchild responded. "What on earth . . ."

Longarm was in no mood to offer an explanation before he'd even had the chance to inspect the room, so he followed Big Mamma down the hallway, and when he entered Milly's room, he could see that the window was still wide open. He went over, stuck his head out, and looked down at a bunch of footprints.

Turning back to the Love Sisters and the Porters, Custis said, "It appears that several people have been out there already, and that sure doesn't help things."

"Who are you?" Alice snapped.

Longarm was tired of acting like a stagecoach driver. "I'm a United States deputy marshal. I was asked to keep my identity a secret and protect you girls."

"I should have known you were a spy," Alice told him, her voice turning contemptuous. "Only, instead of taking care of Milly, you were humping her. Right?"

"Alice!" Big Mamma snapped. "That's enough of that talk."

"Well, it's true, isn't it?"

"Yeah," Longarm said wearily. "Did any of you see a man hanging around here last evening?"

"There were a few men, but they didn't bother us," Esther replied. "They were curious. They just stood around outside the house for a short while, then left. Marshal, all the windows have locks and were locked."

"I saw the locks," he told the minister's wife. "Milly must have opened her window to catch a night breeze."

The Reverend Porter said, "I think we had better get down on our knees right now and pray that girl is safe."

Longarm went over to the bed and stared at the bloodstains on the bedsheets. There were enough to make him fear the worst. "I haven't got time to pray, Reverend," he growled as he hurried past the man and then went outside.

He found nothing in the yard directly behind Milly's bedroom window. But when he began to prowl farther out toward a back alley, he immediately noticed a fresh set of wagon wheels. So fresh that Longarm doubted they were more than a couple of hours old, and so narrow that they would belong to a buggy rather than a heavier buckboard or wagon.

Big Mamma and the others had followed him around the yard, talking too fast and too much, but Longarm had paid them no mind. Now, however, he turned to the Love Sisters and the Porters. "I need everyone to go back to the house and calm down while I try to follow this wagon track."

"Do you want a saddle horse?" the reverend asked.

"It would help."

"I've got one in that old barn. He's not much, but there's a saddle, blankets, and bridle you can also use. I still minister to those who can't come to church because of their poor health, and so I ride a circuit during the week when the weather permits."

Longarm hated to waste the time, but he figured he was probably going to have to cover more ground than he could do practically on foot, so he said, "Saddle me that horse while I have a few words with everyone."

"All right."

As soon as the man was gone, Longarm folded his arms across his chest, studied each of the women, and said, "There's one thing that I need from all of you while I follow those tracks and try to help Milly."

The Love Sisters fell silent and Longarm continued. "I want everyone to go back into the house and stay there until I return. I don't want anyone to say a word about Milly being abducted . . . if in fact she was abducted."

"What else could have happened to her?" Big Mamma asked.

"Milly was a very . . . adventurous young woman and she might have invited a caller into her room," Longarm told them, knowing his words would not sit well.

"You're crazy!" Alice yelled. "Do you think Milly would have knowingly allowed someone to come in her room and hurt her?"

"Of course not. But she could have been fooled and then something unexpected happened."

Big Mamma nodded in agreement. Alice and Elizabeth shook their heads with disbelief, while the reverend's wife just looked scared.

"The reason that it's important we don't say anything just yet is that the very last thing I want is an angry crowd of miners storming around this area looking for that girl and her kidnapper. They'd start drinking, then begin to quarrel and make things all that more difficult."

"I don't see how you can hope to find her," Elizabeth said. "I mean, once those wheel tracks get onto the main road, you won't be able to locate them."

"I might if I hurry," Longarm argued. "From my experience, I'd say those tracks are no more than four or five hours old. The team had two horses, both wearing badly worn-out shoes."

"You can see that?" Alice Fairchild asked, going over to study the tracks.

"Yes," Longarm told her without the slightest bit of hesitation.

"I wish I could go with you," Big Mamma said. "I was less than ten feet down the hall when it happened last night and feel terribly guilty."

"Don't," he said, taking the woman aside and adding in a confidential tone, "My hunch is that Milly allowed the man into her room."

"Why do you say that?"

"Because if he wasn't invited, Milly would have screamed or at least created a disturbance so that someone would come running."

"Unless she was foolish, left the window open, and was knocked unconscious in her sleep before she could yell or fight."

"That is a possibility," Longarm agreed. "But it's the one that I'd rather not consider."

Longarm went back to his room and strapped on his gunbelt. On his way outside, Big Mamma intercepted him, then handed him a Winchester and a sack of extra bullets. "You be careful," she said.

"I always am."

"Do you think she is dead?"

"No," Longarm replied. "I think that some woman-hungry miner saw her climb out of our stagecoach and decided he had to have Milly for himself."

"But—"

Longarm put his arms around Big Mamma. "Just hope for the best. A woman as pretty as Milly will be seen and remembered. So even if I lose the tracks, it shouldn't be long before someone comes and says that they know where she's been taken."

"All right."

"Georgia, you and the Love Sisters came up here wanting to do some charity in order to help women. I'd suggest that you ought to start doing that this very morning. It would take your minds off Milly and you'd feel useful."

"I'm not sure that we could do that with Milly gone and maybe dead."

"Yeah," Longarm said, "I can understand that." He kissed Georgia on the cheek and headed outside, where Reverend Porter was tightening the cinch on his horse. The man had not been exaggerating when he'd said that his horse wasn't worth much. It was an old white gelding with brown speckles. The animal had a jug-head, crooked front legs, and a long, pencil-thin neck.

"He's ugly, all right," Longarm said. "Is he sound?"

"As a dollar," the reverend replied. "He's been shod and has no real bad habits other than he stumbles quite regularly."

"How old is he?" Longarm asked, noting the deep depressions over the gelding's eyes.

"Probably about twenty-five." The man patted the horse affectionately. "I bought Snowball when he was just a youngster, and we've saved a lot of souls and ministered to many, many sick and dying."

Longarm thought that Snowball was ready for the last rites any day now, but said, "I won't push the old fella hard. If the tracks take me far out of Gold Creek, I'll return to the livery and get a younger mount."

"That young lady is what matters most. And besides, you might be surprised at how much stamina Snowball still has in him. This old fella can still climb the steepest trails like a mountain goat."

And he looks like an old mountain goat, Longarm

thought to himself as he jammed his boot into the stirrup and gathered the reins in his hands.

"I ought to lengthen those stirrups," the reverend told him. "Otherwise, you'll chafe the insides of your knees the way they're all bent up."

"I'll be fine," Longarm said, kicking his boots out of the stirrups. "With any luck at all, whoever took Milly did not go very far. I expect she's within a mile or two of us."

The reverend swallowed. "I hold myself to blame for not putting better locks on the windows. Do you think that the young lady has been . . . raped?"

"I wouldn't care to speculate," Longarm replied, almost sure that Milly had in fact been raped. "Just hope for the best."

"And pray," the man told him. "Prayer is all-powerful."

Longarm nodded and rode back to the alley. He leaned a bit out of the saddle and studied the hoofprints, etching their images into his mind. "All right, Snowball. Let's go find whoever was driving that buggy and get Milly back."

The old gelding stamped its foot impatiently and when Longarm gave the animal free rein, Snowball stepped out in a surprisingly lively manner.

The buggy tracks followed a rutted dirt road north about a half mile. Then they angled to the west and joined the main road heading out of Gold Creek up into even higher country. By the time Longarm arrived at the junction of the two roads, it was a little after eight o'clock in the morning and there was a fair amount of traffic obliterating the tracks he followed. Heavy wagons loaded with timber, ore, and all manner of supplies were commonplace, and by nine o'clock, Longarm was out of the saddle and leading Snowball because he often had to kneel down in the dirt and pick out the buggy's tracks and the distinctive hoofprints he followed.

"Hey, mister!" a freighter called as he drew his mules to a standstill. "What are you doing?"

"I'm following the tracks of a buggy," Longarm told the man. "Have you seen one heading north?"

"Nope, and I been on this road since sunrise. Come from Oreville up yonder and over this mountain. You been there before?"

"I have," Longarm replied. "It must be about ten more miles."

"You got that figured right." The mule skinner spat a stream of tobacco at a beetle that was making its way across the road, and drenched the insect, which rolled up in a ball and died, its little legs kicking.

The mules skinner chuckled. "I got the aim on today!"

"You sure do," Longarm said, climbing back on Snowball.

"I ain't seen no buggy, but I did pass a traveling gunsmith driving two horses pullin' what I'd call an enclosed jump-seat wagon."

Longarm was suddenly very interested in the mule skinner. "Did you recognize the man?"

"Sure! He has a wife and two kids, but he's always on the move. The man fixes anything that shoots and also sharpens knifes and axes. His name is . . . let's see now. It's Harley Clum."

"Describe him."

"Say, isn't that Reverend Potter's old Snowball horse?"

"That's right. Tell me about Harley."

"Ain't much to say. He's about your age. Crack shot who sometimes makes side money in shooting matches."

"Is he light- or dark-haired?"

"Light. Got yeller hair and pale blue eyes. Kinda tall and a ladies' man, or so I've heard, despite his poor wife and family. They live in some run-down shack in Oreville while he goes gallivanting all over these mountains. People say that some women who hire him to sharpen their

93

kitchen knives pay Harley a little extra to do a little extra."
The mule skinner winked. "If you catch the drift of my
meaning."

"I do. How long ago did the man pass you?"

"Oh, at least two hours."

"Where does Harley live?"

The mule skinner waved his hand in a circle. "He lives
wherever he finds business. But his place is at the far end
of Oreville. His wife does laundry, cleaning, and cooking
to make money. But Harley is too restless to work a
steady job and he has a bad reputation."

"As a ladies' man."

"As a *hard* man." The driver frowned. "Harley has cut
up more than a few men in his time. He's not only good
with a gun or a rifle, but he's supposed to be a pretty fair
knife fighter."

"Thanks for the information."

"You're welcome. What's the matter? Is your gun nee-
din' a fix?"

"Yeah," Longarm lied, not wanting to spread the news
about Milly's abduction.

"Well, then, Harley Clum is the man you want to see,
and you can probably find him at his shack in Oreville or
in one of their saloons."

"Much obliged," Longarm said.

"Why you ridin' old Snowball? The reverend finally
decide to sell that old bag of bones?"

"No, he just let me borrow his horse."

"You ought to shoot the sorry sonofabitch just for being
so ugly," the mule skinner said as he continued on down
the road.

Longarm didn't bother to reply. He might be entirely
wrong, but he was guessing that Harley Clum was his
man. Dammit, he had to be the one, but surely he
wouldn't take poor Milly to his own shack where he had
a family.

Then he's taking her someplace else to use or to kill, Longarm thought, still able to pick out the gunsmith's wagon tracks. Maybe even to sell to other men who will use Milly for their pleasure and then dump her body down some mine shaft or bury it in the ground.

Longarm was more worried than ever, so he whipped old Snowball into a trot and just hoped he could find Milly before it was too late.

Chapter 9

Longarm pushed the old gelding just as hard as the anim
would go toward Oreville. Snowball was slow, but he w
surprisingly tough and game. The air was thin and col
and the old horse barely broke a sweat.

About three miles south of the mining town, Longa
suddenly drew rein and stared down at the set of ir
wheel tracks he'd been following, which were now vee
ing off the main road onto a dirt track leading into
narrow canyon. Longarm couldn't see a miner's camp
cabin, but he could see smoke drifting lazily into the cle
blue sky about a mile away.

"He must have taken her up that track," Longarm m
tered to himself. "My guess is that he's either got a hid
out shack or a camp up in those trees. I suppose he mig
also have men up there who will pay him to use Milly

Longarm pushed Snowball up the track as fast as t
old animal would go, which was not very fast. Since
was still morning and the shack was hidden up this s
cluded canyon, he was betting that no one would see hi
until he was almost right on top of his quarry. But just
be sure, Longarm reined Snowball off the track and in
the trees, and up a steep, rocky, and twisting game tra

He was doing just fine until the old gelding stumbled and fell hard. Longarm didn't have time to kick out of his stirrups and Snowball smashed down on his leg, pinning him under the old horse's weight.

For a moment, the pain in Longarm's knee was so intense that he lost consciousness. Snowball had landed and slid across on pine needles a few yards down into a little gully so that his legs were uphill and his body on the downside, wedged against a couple of huge pines. The more the old horse thrashed, the more he seemed to press in tight against the trees. And by the time Longarm regained his senses, he was also pinned and in a terrible fix.

"Easy, easy," Longarm grated, his voice thin with pain as he tried to calm the gelding before it went crazy and ground his right lower leg into raw meat and splintered bones. "Take it easy, old horse. We're going to get out of this fix."

Snowball seemed to understand, and he quit thrashing his pencil-thin neck and beating his ugly head against the earth. But the horse was breathing hard and when it rolled its eyes at Longarm, he knew the animal was helpless and terrified. No doubt it had never fallen into this bad of a fix and then been unable to pull itself back to its own feet.

"I don't know what we're going to do," Longarm told the animal as his mind struggled to fight off the pain and come up with a survival plan. "I could draw my gun and fire it to attract help, but Harley Clum would come running and when he found me, I'd be in an even worse mess than I am now."

Longarm fought down the urge to panic as he struggled to drag his leg out from under the horse. But that, he grimly concluded, was going to be impossible. *If I can't get free, I'm going to die right here, up in these lonesome pines. It might be weeks or even months before anyone would discover my body.*

Longarm struggled, but at last faced the fact that unless

Snowball could somehow right himself, nothing was going to change for the better.

"Old horse," he said, "you've got to turn yourself a mite so you can get your legs to the down slope. Otherwise, we could both die on this mountain."

Snowball tried again to right himself. He grunted and groaned, thrashed his legs and slammed his ugly head up and down, but none of it helped until Longarm managed to wiggle his fingers down into his coat pocket and extract his pocketknife. Then, he reached up and sawed through the latigo, cutting loose the saddle.

"That ought to help," he told Snowball. "Try again and you won't have my weight and that of the saddle to lift anymore."

It worked. Unencumbered by the extra weight pinned to his back, Snowball thrashed until one of his back legs struck the pine and he pushed his body half around. Legs now perpendicular to the slope, the animal was able to scramble to its feet, where it snorted and fought for breath, eyes staring suspiciously at Longarm as if he were the cause of this grave misfortune.

Longarm was also free, but his leg had gone numb, and he didn't need to cut his pants open to know that his right knee was either sprained, crushed, or dislocated.

Great. Just great, he thought as he eased into a sitting position and tried to bend the knee. It did bend, but the act itself hurt so much that Longarm broke out in a cold sweat. *So what now? What can I do for myself . . . and for Milly?*

Longarm really didn't have an answer to that, except that he had to try to just do his best in the face of this unexpected catastrophe. So he twisted around, grabbed ahold of a pine tree, and leveraged himself up onto one leg. That accomplished, he eased his weight onto his right leg to learn how much weight it could bear. To his surprise, the right knee held his weight, so he took a few

98

tentative steps, and found that he could walk but it was god-awfully painful.

"Well, Snowball," he said, trembling from his exertions, "we have some tough decisions to make. The first being how am I going to reach that smoke and find out if Milly is still alive."

Longarm studied the saddle, and decided that he had no choice but to knot the latigo together and hope that it would hold his weight while he remounted. Snowball seemed unhurt, though shaken. The white and speckled old gelding kept shaking his head as if he were still in a daze.

"We're going to go busting into that camp up ahead and let the cards fall where they will," Longarm told the horse. "But you have to stand still and let me try and cinch this saddle back down tight and then somehow remount. Otherwise, I'm sunk. Can you understand and will ya at least try not to fall down again?"

Snowball snorted, and Longarm took that as an affirmative.

He tied the latigo, eased Snowball's blanket onto his sweaty back, and was glad that the saddle was both cheap and light as he slung it onto the gelding. Then, he recinched the old horse and turned him on the steep slope so that the animal was on the downslope and mounting was easier.

Longarm made sure that his Winchester was still tied to the saddle, and then he shoved his left boot into the stirrup and gritted his teeth to keep from shouting from the pain as he hauled himself back on top. If Snowball had been feisty or frisky and sidestepped away, Longarm was sure he would have lost his balance and fallen, but the old horse stood like a marble statue.

"Good boy," Longarm told the horse. "You're pig-ugly, but you do have some fine qualities and for that I'm thankful."

Longarm gathered the reins, levered a shell into the Winchester, and laid it across his lap. He checked his six-gun, and decided that he was as ready as he'd ever be for what awaited up this canyon. "Snowball, let's get this over with."

They picked their way another half mile up through heavy brush, still following the game trail, and when they came to the edge of the trees, Longarm drew rein and studied what had once been a mountain man's log cabin up ahead. It had endured many a long, hard Colorado winter, and deep snows had taken their toll. Part of the roof was caved in, and the front door was hanging lopsided on its leather hinges. But whoever was inside had a fire going, and the buggy that he'd followed from Gold Creek was unhitched. Longarm saw that the pair of horses that had pulled the buggy were in a pole corral along with two other saddle horses.

Longarm frowned as he sat hidden in the trees contemplating his next move. *There are probably three men inside. These are poor odds, and I have to do this right or Milly and I will both be killed.*

Had Longarm been in fitter shape, he would have dismounted and crept up to the cabin, hoping to surprise and get the drop on Harley Clum and however many others were inside with Milly. But he wasn't in any shape to do much walking, let alone sneaking up on the shack, so he really had no choice but to ride in and take his chances. Deciding that his best course was to ride slow and get as close to the cabin as possible before he alerted Clum and the others, Longarm holstered his Winchester, tied his reins together, and set the old gelding in motion.

The four horses penned in the corral all threw their heads up and stared at Snowball, and Longarm said a silent but fervent prayer that they would not whinny a greeting and prematurely alert the men inside.

But his prayers were in vain. One of the horses, a palomino, bugled a loud greeting. Longarm knew that would bring someone outside to investigate. A horse didn't whinny without some reason. So he raised his rifle, took aim on the door, and brought Snowball to a standstill so that he could have an accurate first shot.

The grubby fellow who appeared held a six-gun in his fist, but wore no pants or shirt; only a pair of dirty woolen stockings and a very large erection. When he saw Longarm and the Winchester pointed at his chest, he shouted and started to raise his gun and fire, but Longarm drilled him clean, knocking the man back into the cabin. A second man appeared, wild-eyed and equally naked, and he managed to get a shot off before Longarm put a bullet through his gut. The stranger howled and collapsed, arms and legs going every which way.

Longarm dropped the Winchester and booted the gelding straight at the shack. Someone fired at him from a crude window, and Longarm felt a slug punch into the pommel of his saddle. Another bullet struck his gunbelt and empty holster, nearly severing them from his body. Longarm drew his six-gun and returned fire, not expecting to hit his man from the back of a fast-trotting horse, but in the desperate hope that he might at least rattle whoever was trying to kill him.

He thought he heard Milly cry out, but the one with the slug in his gut was still howling so loud that Longarm could not be certain. Then a man bolted out from under a place where the roof had collapsed, and sprinted for the trees. Longarm sawed on his reins and went after the fugitive.

Snowball would not gallop, but the sorry old sonofabitch was a trotting fool and he closed in fast on the fleeing man. Suddenly they were into the pines again, and Longarm was ducking branches and trying to hang on and not be torn from his saddle. He was doing pretty good until Snowball tripped over a rotting log and they both went somersaulting end-over-end. Longarm kicked out of his stirrups and landed on a bed of pine needles. He sledded about twenty feet and his six-gun went flying.

Snowball tried to get up again, but the old horse had broken its right foreleg. Longarm scrambled for his fallen six-gun, but the man he'd been chasing suddenly appeared not twenty feet away. This one had his pants on, but no shoes or shirt. He must have cut the bottoms of his feet in the forest because he was limping.

I am a goner, Longarm thought, reaching for his hideout derringer attached to his watch fob. If he stays back and drills me, I haven't got a chance of hitting him with a two-shot derringer. So I got to draw him in closer.

"Who the hell *are* you?" the man screamed as he cocked back the hammer of his gun. "What the hell did you do that for?"

Longarm was turned on his side, and now he had his derringer ready to fire. "I'm hurt!"

The man fit the description of Harley Clum, and Longarm just knew this was the one that had taken Milly last night. Clum was tall, handsome, and right now he was trembling with rage as he raised his pistol and took careful aim.

"Where is Milly?" Longarm shouted. "She has all my money!"

Clum hesitated and moved closer. "That girl has money?"

"Two thousand dollars."

"She didn't say nothing about no money," Clum spat. "But by God she'll tell me about it when I'm finished with you!"

Longarm knew that he couldn't wait another second. So he rolled hard and fired twice. His first slug missed, but the second struck Harley Clum in the face, obliterating his hate-filled expression. Clum staggered backward, gun hiccuping bullets into the upper reaches of a pine tree as he fell backwards, already dead on his feet.

Longarm dragged himself over to his six-gun, and finally to Snowball, who had a world of suffering in his large brown eyes. "I'm sorry," he said. "Gawdammit, you were a good horse despite being so ugly."

Longarm did the only thing a man could do for a horse in such bad shape with no hope of healing—he shot the gelding between the eyes. Then, he crawled over to his rifle, gathered it up, and pushed himself to his feet. Using the rifle as a cane, he hobbled painfully toward the old log cabin to see if Milly was still alive.

She met him at the edge of the clearing and she was sobbing hysterically. Milly had grabbed a blanket and wrapped it around herself, but there was enough of her body showing to tell Longarm that she had been raped and badly handled. There were purple bruise marks all over the places he could see, and Longarm was sure there were a whole lot more that he could not see.

"Custis!" she sobbed, throwing her arms around his neck. "My God, thank heavens you found and saved me!"

Milly trembled violently, and Longarm would have held her tight, except that he feared letting go of the rifle crutch because then he would most likely fall. His right knee was throbbing, and he was sure that it was badly swollen.

"We're going back to Gold Creek and take care of you," he told the young woman. "Everything is going to be all right."

"I let him into my room. I . . . I must have been out of my mind to do that, but we'd talked in the moonlight for—"

"Shhh," Longarm whispered. "It doesn't matter. You didn't deserve what Clum and those others did to you."

"It was a nightmare."

"I know. But it's over. Help me to the cabin and let's get you cleaned up and then let's get out of here."

"There are two dead men."

"They'll keep," Longarm said grimly. "I'll send someone back for all three later. Let's get that buggy hitched and leave as quick as we can. Everyone back at the Porter house is sure that you are dead."

"I deserve to be," Milly told him. She stepped back, still shaking violently. "I deserved what I got!"

Longarm shook his head. "No, you didn't. You made a stupid mistake and it almost cost you your life."

"And yours."

"Yes," he agreed. "And mine. But everyone makes stupid mistakes. Harley Clum and those others were rotten. If they did you wrong, you can be sure that they've done other women wrong. I say good riddance. The world is better off with them dead."

"Yes," she said nodding her head vigorously. "They were . . . *animals*!"

"It's over," Longarm repeated. "Get dressed and then come and help me hitch up the buggy."

Milly nodded. "I'll never forget this."

"I know. But try."

Milly's entire body shuddered violently. "And I'll never forget how you came and saved my life. You're my hero, Custis."

"We're wasting time. Get dressed and let's leave this place."

Milly turned and went inside. Longarm hobbled over to the corral and found the buggy's harness, which he dragged in among the horses. His knee was a torment and he had to stop every few paces and clear his mind. When he turned around to glance back at the old mountain man's cabin, he saw Milly emerge from its smoke-filled doorway. Then he saw flames licking at the open window, and knew that she had torched the place, maybe to sear it from her memory.

Longarm grabbed ahold of the top of the corral and watched the cabin burn for a while. Then he turned his attention back to the now-nervous horses.

Chapter 10

By the time Longarm and Milly returned to Gold Creek later that day, there was a crowd of anxious men gathered outside the reverend's house, blocking the street. As Longarm drove toward them, a miner shouted, "There she is!"

Suddenly, everyone came running. Longarm pulled up and set the brake, then raised his hands for silence as the men gathered around.

"I guess," he said looking at their grim, worried faces, "you men are wondering what happened last night."

"That's right. One of the boys saw your folks out back of the Reverend's place this morning and we put two and two together. It wasn't hard to figure that one of the girls was hurt or kidnapped."

"Gentlemen," Milly said, raising her chin and meeting their questioning eyes, "as you can see, I'm all right. And I do appreciate your kind concern."

"Miss, we'd like to know who the jasper was that did you wrong," a big, heavy-set man with a red flannel shirt and knee-high black boots said. "We'll hand out the proper justice once we get ahold of him."

"It was a traveling gunsmith, Harley Clum. And as for

justice, that's already been handed out because Harley is dead."

"Are you sure it was Harley?" someone asked. "He was *married*!"

"So I heard," Longarm told the astonished group. "I understand he also has a couple of kids."

"Two young boys," a smallish miner wearing a green cap said. "Harley had a good wife. She wasn't all that pretty, but she was a good woman."

It was Milly's turn to speak. "Then I suggest we all take up a collection for the Clum family."

"Fine idea!" one of the local merchants quickly agreed as he scooped his hat off a balding head and pitched in several greenbacks. "Let's take up a collection for the Widow Clum and her boys!"

The hat went around, and soon returned brimming with cash and coins. It was agreed that a committee would ride over to Oreville this very day and deliver both the bad news and the money.

"Gents," Longarm said, "Miss Milly has had a bad time and she needs to rest and recover. If someone would take this buggy off my hands and see that it gets back to its rightful owner, I'd appreciate it."

He helped Milly down and the crowd parted, men removing their hats as a sign of respect as Milly passed on to the reverend's house, where they were greeted by the Love Sisters and the Porters.

"I sure am glad to see you back," Big Mamma said to Longarm. "What happened to your leg?"

"Long story," he said, coming to rest on the living room couch while Big Mamma and the ladies helped Milly to her room. The ladies looked pale and shocked by Milly's appearance, and Longarm suspected they had already guessed what had happened in that mountain cabin up near Oreville. "Reverend, I have some very bad news. Snowball is dead. He stumbled on a mountain trail and broke his leg. I had no choice but to put him down."

The Reverend Porter looked away for a moment. "As you would expect, I'm deeply saddened by that news. Snowball and I did a lot of good evangelizing here in the Rockies. I like to think that horse had as much to do with saving souls as I did."

"I'll pay you for the animal and tack."

"He was not worth much, but whatever you can spare is appreciated. Mainly, we're just thankful to have Miss Milly back safe and sound." The reverend leaned forward. "Is she . . . all right?"

"I believe she's going to be fine," Longarm replied, hoping that was the case.

Mrs. Porter returned, and looked at her husband. "I know that liquor is the devil's brew for some, but I think the marshal is in pain and could use a good stiff drink."

"I agree," the reverend decided after a moment of deliberation. "Marshal Long, contrary to what you might expect, the missus and I do enjoy a little toddy in the evening. I don't advertise the fact and I don't drink in public, but I am no hypocrite and you are welcome to a generous libation."

"I would very much appreciate that," Longarm said. "When Snowball fell, my leg was trapped under the horse, and I'm afraid that my knee is seriously injured."

"Then we should have a look at it at once," the reverend's wife said. "Just as soon as I bring you a glass of rye whiskey."

When she disappeared, Reverend Porter leaned forward and said, "I suppose a burial service is in order."

"Yes," Longarm said. "One for Harley Clum and also for the other two men that I found with Miss Milly."

Porter's eyes widened. "You killed *three* men?"

"It was them . . . or Milly and me. There was no surrender in any of them, Reverend. I was just lucky to come through it alive and to be able to save that girl."

Porter shook his head. "I had better go at once and see what I can do. Oreville has a minister, but he is a man of intemperate ways and not much to my liking."

Longarm gave the man directions to the burned-down cabin, explaining that two of the dead men were most likely cremated. Before Porter could voice his unhappiness at this news, Longarm asked, "Do you know Mrs. Clum and her boys?"

"I do. They are Christian people. I understand that a collection was taken up outside for the poor woman and her children."

"That's right."

"I'll take up another among my brethren. Even so, I'm afraid that the woman is in for a very difficult time of it. Harley Clum wasn't much of a husband, but I am sure that he did help support his family."

Longarm had nothing to say about that, and when Mrs. Porter returned with a water glass full of whiskey, he pretended not to notice how the reverend's eyebrows shot up with surprise and mild disapproval. Longarm thanked the dear woman and drained half the glass in three big swallows, savoring the warmth that immediately flooded down into his belly.

"Now," Mrs. Porter said, "would you please remove your boots and pants so that I can attend to your injury?"

"Mrs. Porter, I think that I can take care of it myself."

"Nonsense."

"Let me try," Longarm said. "I think it might just need a bit of rest."

"Esther," the reverend said, "why don't you let the marshal do as he wishes."

"Very well, if that is his choice. But false modesty is no virtue, Marshal Long. It says in the Bible that—"

"Esther," Reverend Porter said with a slight edge to his voice. "Why don't you come with me to Oreville. I'm sure that you can also be of service to the widowed Mrs. Clum and her grieving children."

The woman seemed to think that was a fine idea, and there was no more discussion on the matter. Longarm hobbled to his room with his glass of whiskey, and closed the door. He slowly removed his pants, and was shocked at the amount of swelling in his knee and at its dark-purplish coloration. Longarm wondered if he could somehow get some ice, and then decided that it was too late for that to do much good anyway.

"Custis," Big Mamma whispered, opening his door to peek inside. "Are you decent?"

"No, but come in anyway," he said.

When Big Mamma closed the door and then saw his leg, she took a sharp intake of breath. "Oh, my gosh! You really did a job on yourself."

"No, Snowball did."

"Is it broken or dislocated?"

Longarm shook his head. "But I'm really going to be hobbling for at least a couple of days. How is Milly?"

"She's been pretty badly abused. I'm amazed that she is not in hysterics. That girl has more spunk and steel in her spine than I thought."

"That's my opinion as well," Longarm said, draining his whiskey. "So I guess the question now is, what do we do next? I'm thinking that this mission has failed."

"Oh?"

"Sure," Longarm said. "Three of the Love Sisters have quit and Milly has been raped and beaten. What is going to befall us next?"

"I don't know."

"If you get someone to hitch the stagecoach up, we can head down the mountain for Denver first thing in the morning."

"You can head down the mountain, but Milly, Elizabeth, Alice, and myself won't be going with you."

"You're staying?"

"We just talked it over, and I didn't even try to convince the Love Sisters to see it through. But that is exactly what they wanted and I'm all for it."

Longarm was caught by surprise. He'd expected all of the remaining Love Sisters to give up. "So what would you have me do?"

"Take us to Oreville," Big Mamma told him. "We want to pay a visit to that poor Widow Clum and her children. We think she ought to be the first one that we really help with the money we have to give."

"What about Milly?"

"What about her?"

Longarm frowned. "Won't it be a little difficult for her and Mrs. Clum, given what happened today?"

"Yes," Big Mamma admitted. "It probably will, but if you really understood women, you'd know that they will probably find a healing and forgiveness in each other. Milly needs to do this very much."

"Then that's what we'll do," Longarm said.

Big Mamma studied the knee. "You need ice to take down that swelling. There must be an icehouse in Gold Creek. I'll find it."

Longarm smiled. "I'd sure appreciate it if you also found me a bottle of whiskey."

"I can do that. And will we drink it together?"

"In the reverend's house?"

"Or on his back lawn, in poor Snowball's empty barn, or wherever you prefer," Big Mamma said with a mischievous grin.

Longarm thought about it for a moment. "My leg is killing me, but the ice and the whiskey will make it better. Let's tie one on in the barn and offer a couple of toasts to old Snowball. He was the clumsiest, stumbliest horse I ever rode, but he was long on heart. I feel worse about losing him than I do about killing them three sonsabitches I found at the cabin."

Big Mamma lightly brushed her fingers over Longarm's knee. "How is your butt wound?"

110

"I hadn't even thought about it."

"Roll over and let me have a look."

"Aw . . ."

"Come on!"

Longarm rolled over and felt Big Mamma examining his buttocks. "Looks nice."

"Really?"

"It's almost healed."

"Well, that is some small measure of good news," he said. "I don't know when I've ever been so banged up."

"Custis, I'm gonna draw you a warm bath and tonight we'll make everything feel better out in the horse barn."

"Can I take that as a promise?" he asked.

"You sure can."

Longarm grinned through his pain, and figured that although this day had started out all wrong, it might end up just fine after all.

That night Longarm and Big Mamma set about to get more than just a little tipsy as they sat in a pile of hay and talked about life and love. Before the bottle was half empty, Big Mamma was kissing Longarm and ministering to his injuries in a way unlike any nurse or doctor.

"I think that we need to make love," she said, pushing him down and kissing his mouth. "In fact, I'm *sure* that we do."

"Georgia," he told her, "I'm a little drunk and I'm in real sorry condition."

She reached into his pants and her big hand closed gently on his rod. "Is there anything wrong with this?" she asked.

"No, but . . ."

"Why don't you just stop worrying about it?" she asked. "Let me do all the work and you just lay still and enjoy it. You can make it up to me when you're feeling fitter."

"That sounds like a fair trade to me," he said, feeling his manhood stiffen with anticipation.

Big Mamma leaned over and took his manhood in both hands, and began to lick its head with her tongue and stroke his shaft. "Are you feeling any better now, darlin'?"

"Yeah, quite a bit!"

"Good." Her mouth closed over the head of his rod, warm and wet. Longarm sighed with pleasure, and then she began to move her lips up and down, tongue licking every inch of his now-throbbing manhood. "How's this?"

"Don't stop."

"Darlin'," she breathed, "we are just getting started."

Big Mamma worked Longarm up and down with her lips and tongue until he was ready to bust. Then she removed her blouse and bodice and shook her huge, luscious breasts over his face. Longarm couldn't believe the size of those golden melons. They were enormous, but firm and perfectly shaped, with large, dark nipples that he was soon ravishing with his own mouth.

When the big, beautiful woman began to moan and wiggle her bottom, Longarm thrust upward and she settled down on him like a hen on a nest. Longarm groaned and she whispered, "How's your knee and buttocks feeling now?"

"What buttocks? What knee!"

She giggled and began to shake and churn herself all over him, until Longarm growled and grabbed ahold of her plunging buttocks and impaled her mightily.

"Oh, my goodness gracious!" Big Mamma exclaimed. "Milly, if you can hear me now . . . I forgive you for having this man!"

Longarm laughed, and then he rolled Big Mamma over in the hay and gave her every inch of what he had to offer . . . which must have been enough because when he was finished with the woman, she was thrusting like a steam engine and screeching like a train whistle deep, deep into the night.

Chapter 11

They left Gold Creek at eight o'clock the following morning, and the Love Sisters were in a somber mood.

"You ladies feeling all right?" Longarm called down from his driver's seat to the three women inside the coach.

"Hell, no!" Elizabeth shouted back. "Milly was raped and beaten. What kind of a stupid question is that!"

Longarm glanced sideways at Big Mamma, who gave him a look that said his question was indeed stupid. "What we need to do is get them involved with helping the mining women like we first intended," she said. "I'm hoping that will happen as soon as we reach the town of Oreville."

"Yeah," Longarm said. "But what about Harley Clum's wife and kids?"

"I've been thinking about that," Big Mamma answered. "Milly says that she wants to meet and offer them help."

"It could really hurt instead."

"I know that, but it's important to Milly. She feels . . . kind of responsible for all those deaths."

"That doesn't make any sense."

"Sense or not," Big Mamma said, "that's the way Milly feels. She believes that if she'd been more prudent and locked her window, none of this would have happened. Now, she's been scarred and there is a widow in Oreville with no husband."

"Who is better off without him."

"True. But she might have loved Harley Clum, and what about her sons? Are they to grow up without a father?"

"A father who would do what Harley did to Milly isn't worthy of the title."

"Custis, be honest. Have you ever thought of fatherhood?"

Longarm swallowed hard. "There have been more than a few times when some gal has tried to pin a pregnancy on me so we'd get hitched."

"Maybe you *were* the father."

"Nope. I checked, and in every case the woman had been with other men more'n me. Either that or she wasn't pregnant at all."

"You'd make a fine father."

"No, I wouldn't. I'd be gone all the time on my job. Or else I'd start feeling so guilty about being gone that I'd quit being a marshal, and then I'd have to have some regular work that I most likely would hate."

Big Mamma looked away from him, and was silent as they rolled along during the next few minutes. Finally, she said, "We both know that most things in life have advantages and disadvantages. Sure, you'd miss this job, but it's been my experience that men often think that they are born to only this thing or that thing. Then, when something happens and they have to do something different on account of they got fired, or their employer went broke, or they just got too old and hurt . . . they find something else and like it about as well or not."

"Are you talking about some of those prizefighters that you knew?"

"As a matter of fact, I am."

"That figures. I can't understand why a man would ever want to toe the mark and then stand in a ring before a crowd of screaming men shouting for his blood. When I have to fight, I want it over quick. No rules. Just win however easy and fast that I can and be done with that trouble."

"Fisticuffs is an art."

"If you're saying there is skill involved, then I agree. But mostly what I've seen in prize rings is just two poor fellas pounding the living hell out of each other, trying to win a few dollars. I intend no disrespect to your late husband or his friends, but prizefighting is a blood sport."

"Tell me about Oreville," Big Mamma managed to say.

"It's just another wild mining camp. Got maybe five or six saloons and a couple of big whorehouses. There's a few hotels and cafes, an assay office, and a mercantile. Harness and saddle shop, blacksmith, livery, and feed store."

"Tell me about the houses of ill repute."

"I never visited either of 'em," Longarm said.

"That's not hard to believe."

Longarm suppressed a smile. "I don't know if I should take that as an insult or a compliment."

"Take it as a compliment," she told him. "A man as big and handsome as you shouldn't have to pay for what women gladly will provide you for free."

Now he did smile. "Is that your way of saying you enjoyed it last night and wouldn't mind a repeat?"

"Nice guess. What are the women that work in them like?"

"You mean, are they happy?"

"Yes."

"I can't answer that question, Georgia. But from what I've seen, I'd say not. Most of them are in it just for the money. Most drink way too much liquor, and some use opium and other things that make 'em sick. And they get

115

the French disease and that's the end of them."

"They die?"

"They suffer," Longarm told her. "I know some that have died, but most just seem to age real fast. It's a bad way to live. For the first few years, the youngest and the prettiest are the toast of these mining towns and they can't hardly spend their money fast enough. But they get beat up and cut up, and some commit suicide when they know that their best time has passed and they have to start lowering the price of their bodies."

"It's the same back East. I've seen it."

"Then you know that you and three idealistic women who call themselves the Love Sisters can't change a thing."

"Not true," Big Mamma said. "We may not change much, but we can save a few and that would be worthwhile."

"For a woman who has seen the underbelly of prizefighting, you still have some sugary notions."

"Custis, it's because I've seen the hard side of life for both men and women that I believe we can all make changes for the better. And I suspect that part of the reason that you like being a United States marshal is that you feel the same way."

"Naw," he snorted. "I just work for the money."

Big Mamma jabbed Longarm in the ribs with her elbow. "Don't you dare try and tell me that because I know it's not true."

When they came to the little wagon track leading off the main road up to the cabin where Milly had been taken, Longarm slapped the reins against his team of horses and made them move on past in a hurry. He couldn't see the cabin because it was too far up the canyon, but he could see fresh tracks and suspected that a party of men from Gold Creek had gone up there to do the burying.

116

A few hours later, they began to pass some of the local mining operations, and then they rolled down into a little valley surrounded by high, snow-clad mountain peaks. It was a beautiful setting, but Longarm knew that the winters up in this high country could be extremely harsh.

They saw a boy tending a few sheep, and his dog, a large tan and white animal, barked a warning. Big Mamma waved at the kid and received the same in return. A pair of miners were walking down the road in their direction, and when they saw that Big Mamma was a handsome woman, they stopped and grinned.

"Mornin', miss!" one of them said. "How come you're dressed up in a man's clothes and ridin' shotgun? Don't seem right for a woman as pretty as yourself to be doin' a man's work . . . even if you are bigger'n most men."

"I'm doing what I please," she told them. "How are you doing?"

The other miner removed his hat and said, "A lot better now that I've seen the face of an angel."

Longarm almost burst out laughing, but thought better of it when Big Mamma blushed and said, "Compared to the ladies inside this coach, I'm nothing special. Are you finding any gold?"

"We sure are! Are the ladies inside gonna work at the Calico Cat, or the Speckled Bird?"

Big Mamma's smile died. "Are those houses of sin?"

"Uh . . ." One of the miners paused. "Meaning that the women aren't going to work in them whorehouses?"

"Exactly."

"Well, miss, if they didn't come to please the men . . . then what are you comin' here for?"

"We want to help the downtrodden women of this town," Big Mamma said earnestly. "But first we want to visit Harley Clum's wife and children. Can you tell us where they live?"

"Harley was killed!"

"We know that," Big Mamma replied in a patient voice. "Now where does his family live?"

"Up the road about a half mile. You'll see an old run-down shack on the left in the pines with a big clothesline of wash hangin' out to dry."

"Thank you."

The pair bowed, wished them a good day, and continued on their way toward Gold Creek. As they passed the stagecoach, Longarm overheard one of the men say, "What would ladies want to come to Oreville for if not to work at the Speckled Bird or the Calico Cat?"

"Beats the hell outta me," the other said. "Ladies are useless in a miners' camp."

"Yeah, but maybe they'll get ruined quick."

"I sure hope so. But could be I'll go see Mrs. Clum now that Harley is dead."

Their voices soon faded and Longarm could hear no more of their lively conversation.

"Shall I stop?" Longarm asked, pulling the stage up in front of the Clum shack. "Might be best to first go into town and get our rooms."

"I agree."

But just as Longarm was about to drive on, Milly stuck her head out of the window and yelled, "Is that where Mrs. Clum and her boys live?"

"That's what we were told."

Milly threw the door open. "I'm going in there right now."

Big Mamma started to protest. "Milly, I . . ."

But the young woman was already out of the stagecoach and marching up to the door with Elizabeth and Alice Fairchild hurrying along behind.

"I don't know about this," Big Mamma said, looking worried as she climbed down from the driver's seat and went after the Love Sisters. "Custis, wait there for us!"

"I'm not going anywhere," Longarm shouted in reply.

The door to the shack opened, but Longarm couldn't see what was going on since the women were all crowded around the front of the shack. But he could see they were talking, and then the Love Sisters turned around and came back to climb inside the coach. When Big Mamma was seated next to him, Longarm asked, "Well? What did the man's widow have to say?"

"She wasn't there. Mrs. Clum is working at a restaurant called the Silver Spoon. Her oldest boy gave us directions. Let's go find it."

Longarm put the team of horses in motion and they entered Oreville. It was even smaller and less prosperous-looking than Gold Creek. As they drove up the main street of town, miners came out of saloons to wave and to shout their greetings. Some rushed out and tried to talk the Love Sisters into jumping into their arms.

"This is a rough town," Big Mamma said with her lips pursed together tightly. "We're going to have to watch those girls like we were hawks or we'll have another mess like we did yesterday."

"I agree." Longarm raised a hand and pointed to the Silver Spoon. "You want me to stop there?"

"I'd rather it wait a day or two, but Milly is determined to apologize and help Mrs. Clum. You should have seen the inside of their shack."

"Pretty awful, huh?"

"It was terrible. That family is living in squalor. I saw light coming through cracks in the board walls and the roof. I didn't know that people could be so poor."

"Well," Longarm said, "now you do know, so do what you can to change things for the better."

"We don't have enough money to help everyone, but we'll do the best we can," Big Mamma told him as their stagecoach came to a stop before the restaurant.

Once again the Love Sisters piled out of the stagecoach, and practically had to fight their way through the excited pack of miners. Longarm shook his head, not thinking there was much that he could do to help.

He waited fifteen minutes in front of the Silver Spoon, all the while answering questions about the Love Sisters. When he finally managed to convince the miners that the girls he'd delivered were not whores but missionaries, they were sorely disappointed.

"Hell of a thing for those pretty women to come all the way up here just to see if *other women* can be helped!" one angry miner complained. "Why, we take care of the women of this town ourselves and we sure don't need no help."

"Maybe not, but the Love Sisters aren't here to help anyone who doesn't want or need their help."

"You screwed any of 'em yourself?" one of the men asked hopefully.

Longarm's voice turned hard. "Mister, I'm going to pretend that I didn't hear you ask me that question. Because, if I did, I'd climb down from this coach and knock the hell out of you!"

Actually, his threat was somewhat of a bluff. Given his injured knee, just climbing up and down the side of this coach was an ordeal.

The Silver Spoon did have a couple of front windows, but they were so grimy that Longarm couldn't see what was going on inside. However, all turned out well because the front door opened and Milly came out leading a small, weary-looking woman by the hand. Tears were streaming down all of their faces as they escorted Mrs. Clum up to the stagecoach and helped her inside.

When Big Mamma rejoined Longarm, he asked, "What happened in there?"

"When we first came inside, and the owner realized that we weren't going to order anything to eat, he started giving Mrs. Clum a lot of guff. Milly lit right into him, and then the man fired Mrs. Clum and told us to all get out!"

120

"She lost her job?"

"That's right," Big Mamma said. "But we told her she could be a Love Sister and help us help others."

"What about her two boys?" Longarm asked.

"There's no reason why a Love Sister can't be a Love Mother, is there?"

"No, but . . ."

"And anyway, I said that you'd be happy to sort of help take them under your wings until other arrangements could be made."

"You what!"

"I said you'd help with the boys a little," Big Mamma repeated. "Why? Is there something so terrible about that?"

"Well . . . well, that's not my job!"

"Stop shouting. Let's find a hotel and we can talk about this later."

"Georgia, I'm not cut out to be a father."

"That's what you keep saying." She chuckled. "The boys are John and Ted. They're ten and seven. Seemed like nice enough boys to me. Oh, and we're going to take them out of that shack."

"To live with me?"

Big Mamma nodded. "Seemed a reasonable thing to do."

"Well, it isn't!"

"Why are you getting so upset? I thought you'd enjoy helping a couple of boys instead of playing nursemaid to the Love Sisters."

Longarm was seething. "I just like to make my own damn decisions!"

"Well, sorry, Custis. But you'll do fine whether you think so or not. Now let's find us a good hotel and quit this bickering. I'm feeling good about what just happened. And you know why?"

When Longarm refused to answer, Big Mamma said,

"The reason why I'm suddenly feeling better is that I was proud of Milly, Elizabeth, and Alice when they went into that cafe and stood up for poor Mrs. Clum. The woman is so downtrodden and depressed she started crying, and that made the Love Sisters furious. They lit into that fella who was givin' her a bad time, and I thought they were going to claw his eyes out . . . which he would have deserved."

Longarm put the coach into motion. He was glad that Milly was feeling better and sure wished he could say the same. But the truth of it was that he had never been real comfortable around young kids . . . especially boys, who were generally as sneaky and mean as wild weasels.

Dammit, he thought, six weeks of paid vacation isn't enough for what I'm having to put up with on this assignment.

Chapter 12

Longarm was enjoying a huge breakfast the next morning and finishing off his second cup of coffee when Big Mamma barged into the cafe. "So there you are! I've been looking all over town for you this morning."

"Given the size of Oreville, you shouldn't have had much looking to do," he told her. "Sit down. Are you hungry?"

"As a matter of fact I am. That boardinghouse where we're staying offered up a little bitty breakfast of toast and oatmeal. I hate oatmeal and the toast was burned." She looked down at his nearly clean plate. "How was *your* breakfast?"

"Excellent. I had ham, eggs, and potatoes with sour-dough biscuits and gravy."

Big Mamma swallowed and licked her lips. "Hey!" she shouted, turning toward the kitchen. "I'll have the same as my man!"

"Comin' up!"

"Your man?" Longarm asked.

"Why not? We had great lovemaking, didn't we?"

Longarm brushed back the tips of his lush mustache. "No complaints on my side, Georgia."

"Mine neither. So why don't we do it again tonight?"

Longarm almost choked on his coffee. "Jeezus," he said, coughing, "you sure don't mince words."

"You ought to know that by now," she told him as she grabbed his fork and spread a piece of fat he'd carved off his slice of ham. Jamming the fat into her mouth, she chewed a moment, then said, "The Love Sisters had a meeting already this morning and guess what?"

"What?"

"We're going to call an assembly of all the downtrodden women of Oreville to see what can be done to improve their lot."

"You're not wasting any time."

"Nope," Big Mamma agreed. "Miss Alice is writing up a piece for the newspaper and—"

"Don't mean to rain on your parade, but I doubt that there is a newspaper in Oreville."

This bit of news momentarily threw Big Mamma off, and it took her a moment to recover. "Do you think there is a printer who would do some flyers for us to hand out and tack up?"

"I expect not."

"Then we'll have to compose them by hand. That shouldn't be too difficult. Now, do you know of a hall that we could rent?"

Longarm considered the question. He'd been in Oreville a time or two and now that he thought about it, he realized that there weren't any meeting halls. "Sorry, but I expect not."

Big Mamma sighed. "I'm not getting much help or encouragement here. What about a church? We are sisters of mercy and charity. We could rent a church for just one or two evenings."

"There's only one church in this town," the cook said as he arrived to pour Big Mamma a cup of thick, black coffee. "And it ain't much. The Reverend Jacob Haskell isn't a man who likes to make accommodations contrary to his set ways."

"I think he will change his mind if we offer him a nice donation."

"He might," the cook conceded as he wiped his hands on his greasy apron. "You are a handsome woman, but you sure are a big'un."

"Thank you," Big Mamma said without much enthusiasm. "And right now I have a big appetite, so don't hold back on the eats."

"No, ma'am. I'll fill your belly till you can't eat no more. Won't take me but a few minutes to bring you a plate."

When the cook left, Big Mamma turned to Longarm. "Have you gone out to see the Clum boys yet?"

"Of course not. It's still early."

"Well, we told Helen Clum that you'd be along to take her boys fishing or something."

"I don't like to fish."

"Pretend you do! Custis, you might not have been able to see those boys when we pulled up in front of their shack, but they were a sad pair. Skinny but clean. Dressed in rags that had been mended over and over. The boys need haircuts and they need some shoes." Big Mamma reached into her purse. "Here is some money. You buy 'em some good shoes and clothes and then whatever pleases them."

Longarm shook his head. "Don't you understand that this won't work because I'm the one that gunned down their father?"

"I agree that could be a problem."

" 'Could be'!" Longarm shouted. "Are you crazy? Those two boys will want to kill me."

"I doubt that. You see, Helen has welts on her back from being beaten by her husband, and she broke down last night and told us that her boys have the same. So the

125

way I view this is that you did those kids a big favor by killing Harley Clum."

Longarm scowled. "Georgia, can't somebody . . . anybody else do this? I'm just not cut out to—"

"How do you know you aren't until you give it a try? Try it out for a day or two, and if the boys don't forgive you for their father's death, then we'll make other arrangements. But that doesn't seem like too much to ask, does it?"

"I'm a United States deputy marshal, not a nursemaid."

"These are *good* boys."

"Sure, but I'm here to protect you and the Love Sisters, not—"

"We'll be all right for a couple of days. I'm asking you to do this as a favor to me and Helen Clum, but also as a way to sort of show those boys that all men aren't vicious and no-accounts like their father."

"Okay," Longarm snapped. "I'll walk over there this morning and have a talk with the boys. But I'm gonna tell them what happened out at that shack."

"Not about Milly!"

"I have to," Longarm said. "They're gonna hear about it anyway, and they might as well get the truth instead of what someone dreams up to tell 'em. It's either done straight up and honest, or I won't go out there at all."

"You win."

"I don't think so," Longarm replied as he stood up and dropped change on the table. "I think I've been losing ever since I agreed to take this assignment."

"Then quit, damn you!" Big Mamma shouted. "If you don't want to help us out, we're better off without you."

For a moment, they glared at each other, each ready to say things better left unsaid. Then Longarm wheeled around and barged out of the restaurant. He'd go see the Clum kids and tell them the truth about what he'd done and why there'd been no choice but to kill their father.

• • •

"Hello the house!" he yelled from outside. "Mrs. Clum? Boys!"

The door opened and Helen Clum appeared. Longarm was surprised, and would have hardly recognized the young widow. Her hair was washed and combed, and one of the Love Sisters had given her a pretty dress and shoes. Helen Clum still had a wary and weary look about her, but she was scrubbed clean and was actually quite attractive. Too small and skinny to Longarm's way of thinking, but definitely attractive.

"Marshal Custis Long?"

He swept off his hat. The boys were nowhere in sight, but he suspected they were just inside, watching and listening. "Mrs. Clum, could we step out a ways and have a few words in private?"

"Of course."

When they reached an empty and sagging pole corral, Longarm turned to face the anxious young widow. "First off, I want to say how sorry I am about—"

"Stop," she told him in a quiet but firm voice. "You don't need to explain or to apologize. Harley was a bad man, and I'd be lying to you if I said that I was grieving his death. Matter of fact, I feel as if I've just escaped from a prison. From a living Hell, if you will excuse my language."

Longarm heaved a deep sigh of relief. "I'm glad to hear that. But taking a life, even the life of a no-good man, is never a thing to feel good about. And those other two men might have had wives like you and kids like your boys."

"They didn't," Helen Clum said. "They were loners, thieves and worse. Marshal, I have no tears to shed over the death of my husband. I married Harley when I was fourteen to escape a father that beat and abused me in ways unspeakable. My mother didn't dare to try to shield

127

me and when I tried to protect my sons, I learned why. Harley beat all of us and . . . and he *enjoyed* it."

Longarm stood mute, not knowing what to say but hearing the woman's pain. "What about me and the boys?" he finally stammered. "I don't know if it's such a good idea for me to be around them, seeing as how I shot their father."

"I think they'll look at you as a hero, just the way Milly and I do."

Longarm was a strong man, physically as well as emotionally, but this frail woman's words cut him to the quick. "Well," he said, "I've been told that maybe I ought to start out by taking those boys fishing."

"They're good at it."

"I'm not."

"Then," Helen said, "perhaps they'll teach you a thing or two. Do you hunt?"

"Only men," he said, instantly regretting his frankness.

"My boys hunt squirrels for the pot and about anything else that they can bring down with an old Indian rifle that doesn't shoot straight. We're low on food and you might take a good rifle along just in case you come upon some game for my stewing pot."

"Like a buck."

"Or a doe or even a porcupine. We aren't in any position to be choosy."

"Yes, ma'am, but I don't know that I'd want to try to butcher a porcupine."

"The boys often do it. We eat possum when we get the chance, and also birds and wild berries. We do what we must do to stay alive."

"Could be things will get a lot better for you soon."

"You mean with the Love Sisters?"

"That's right."

Helen smiled. "They actually invited me to be one, but

I said no. I've got too many responsibilities, and now I don't even have a job at the cafe."

"I expect something better will come along," Longarm told her, wanting to sound encouraging.

"Maybe." Helen forced a smile. "Why don't you go meet John and Ted, while I go into town to help the Love Sisters in whatever way I can."

"Whatever you say."

Helen actually giggled.

"What's funny?"

"For a man to say that to a woman like me sounds so . . . so strange that I had to laugh. 'Anything you say.' I . . . well, I don't believe you in the first place, but I sure do appreciate you being such a gentleman. Do you like boys?"

"Not particularly."

"And so honest! Well, I think you'll like my sons. They're good boys. Not a drop of their father in their blood . . . I hope. Good luck, Marshal Long, and thank you again for freeing us from Hell."

"Wait a minute," he said as she turned to walk into town. "Where are they?"

"In the cabin. I told them to tidy things up so you didn't think we were slovenly and had no pride."

"All right."

Longarm managed a hopeful smile, and then he headed back to the house. Even the old mountain man cabin where he'd killed Harley Clum and his friends a day earlier had seemed like a mansion in comparison to this rundown shack. It had no front window, and someone had laid an uneven patch of logs and tried to build a small porch, but it was hanging lopsided and in danger of collapse. This place was constructed of cut lumber that had long ago warped so that there were gaps everywhere that were stuffed with rags and nailed over with flattened tin cans. In truth, Longarm thought that the shack was so pathetic, it would have even put a hound dog to shame.

"Hello in there?"

John came out ahead of his younger brother. They were gangly and thin, but scrubbed clean and wearing nervous smiles.

Longarm stepped up to the rickety porch and extended his hand to the ten-year-old first. "My name is Marshal Custis Long. What's yours?"

The lad threw back his shoulders. "John Clum, sir. And this is my brother, Teddy. Theodore Clum, actually."

The smaller boy nodded as if to assure Longarm that his older brother had gotten the introduction right.

"There's something I need to tell you right now," Longarm said. "In case you didn't know, I'm the one that shot and killed your father. I didn't want to, but if I had not, he would have killed me. There were two others that I also killed, but from what your mother tells me, they were completely of no account."

Longarm studied their faces. John was the handsomer lad, but Ted was the studier-looking of the pair, with penetrating dark eyes. "I thought you boys would want to know about what happened and why."

"No, sir," Ted told him. "We'd rather just go hunting or fishing and forget all about our pa."

"I agree," John said with a serious expression. "He wasn't much good to us and he was terrible to Mamma."

"But he taught us how to fish and hunt a little," Ted added.

"Yes," John agreed. "He was a good shot and he could make fishing flies and catch us a bunch most any time he put his mind to work."

"But he liked to drink and smoke more than fish or hunt." Ted hitched up his pants, which were fastened at the waist by a belt made out of bridle reins. "But that's all over now, isn't it."

"It is," Longarm said.

John shifted his bare feet in the dirt and tried to say something, but seemed to be having a difficult time.

"What is it, John?"

"Well, sir. I was wondering where Pa's body is right now. Maybe he ought to have a decent burial. Might be that God can forgive him even if Mamma can't."

"Do you boys want to see him buried?"

"Not me," Ted quickly replied. "I don't ever want to see his face again, but I don't want wild animals to eat him either."

"That won't happen," Longarm assured the younger boy. "Your father will get a Christian burial. Have you heard of Reverend Porter over in Gold Creek?"

Both boys nodded.

"He's going to take care of things," Longarm told them.

"Sir, would you like to go fishing now?" John asked. "We can show you a good trout stream not far away. Most of the time we can catch a few fish there."

"Sure," Longarm replied. "You boys get your poles and I'll just come along and watch."

"We got Pa's pole for you," John said. "Might as well use it as not. Three fishing have a better chance of havin' supper on the table than just two."

Longarm wasn't a big fish eater. In fact, he preferred most any kind of meat over fish, but now he chose to keep that his secret. "Trout are tasty. All right. Get the poles and whatever else we need and let's see if we can catch a few."

The boys dashed into the shack, and emerged a moment later with three cane poles all rigged and ready to go.

"What," Longarm asked, "are we going to use for bait?"

"Worms and grubs." Ted held up a can for Longarm's inspection. "See?"

Longarm saw the little creatures writhing among the

dirt and dung that filled the can. "Looks like they'll do, all right. Fat and juicy."

"They're skinnier than I am," Ted replied. "But the fish like 'em just fine."

"That's what counts. Are we all set to go then?"

"What about a rifle?" John asked. "We got one, but it ain't much use. Thought you'd bring a rifle in case we come upon a deer."

"Next time I will," Longarm said, patting his side arm.

"How come you wear that hogleg backwards?" Ted asked.

"That's just the way I was taught and I like it fine now."

"Can you shoot it fast and straight?"

"When I have to."

"I'd like to see you shoot something."

But Longarm shook his head. "I was also taught not to draw or fire my gun unless I needed to kill something or someone."

"But didn't you ever practice on cans, bottles, and such?" John asked.

"Well, yes, but . . ."

"I sure would like to see you shoot something fast," Ted repeated. "If you weren't any good, my pa would have killed you dead."

Longarm shrugged and turned to look at the surrounding forest. "Okay. What shall I shoot?"

"How about a pine cone off'n a tree?" John suggested. "Pa could hit one most of the time."

"No, he couldn't," Ted argued. "He'd get drunk and keep shooting until he hit something by accident."

The boys started to wrangle, so Longarm drew his gun, spotted a fat pine cone, and shattered it to bits with his first shot.

"Wow!" John said.

"Gosh," Ted breathed. "You mean to hit that one?"

"I did."

"Gosh," he repeated. "You sure are good."

Longarm decided to holster his gun while he was still ahead of the game. "Let's go catch some fish."

"Now you're talking," Ted said, striding off a footpath that led uphill into the heavy forest.

That afternoon turned out to be one of the best and most enjoyable that Longarm had spent in months. The Clum boys were all business, and when Longarm got bored with fishing early, they took his pole and added it to their own. There was no idle conversation. The boys were excellent fishermen. Little Ted especially. He caught five, none of them worthy of a prize, but all of a good eating size. John caught four, and the boys had their fishing line full by three o'clock.

"You shoot a lot better than you fish," Ted told him. "What's the matter, don't you like it?"

"I'd rather take a nap or read a book," Longarm confessed.

"That won't put supper on your table," John told him with a frown of disapproval. "You have to work at it or you don't catch nothing and the fish will just steal all your good bait."

"I suppose that is true," Longarm agreed. "How would you boys like to go into town with me after we eat those fish?"

"For what?"

Longarm withdrew the money that Big Mamma had given him that morning. He had added some of his own. "I was thinking that you might like to visit that mercantile and have some candy and maybe buy something."

"Something," John asked, "like new fishing line?"

"Or something else that we might see of interest."

"We don't have any cash money, sir." Ted's lower lip pushed out. "We never have any money."

"Then I'll do the buying for all of us," Longarm told

the lads. "Starting with some hard candy . . . if they have any."

"Mr. Trimble carries licorice and rock candy sweeter than anything," Ted said, unable to keep the excitement out of his voice. "And he has bottles of sarsaparilla."

"Then we'll each have one," Longarm declared, wondering how long it had been since he'd tasted the stuff.

The boys were on their feet in an instant. Each grabbed an end of their fishing line, and it was all that Longarm could do to keep up with them as they rushed back down the mountainside to their shack.

They cleaned the fish and started an outdoor cooking fire using pine needles and cones, then adding bark and finally wood. On an old wire grill, they laid the fish out, and then ran into the shack and cut potatoes. Thirty minutes later, Longarm was enjoying his supper on a cracked tin plate.

"You like 'em?" Ted asked hopefully.

"Sure do."

"Thought you would," John said. "Potatoes are good too, huh?"

"Yes, but they could use a little salt and pepper."

"Maybe we can get some at the store," Ted suggested.

Longarm took another drink of water and nodded his head. "I think we can do that easy. Anything else you need?"

"No, sir."

"What about milk?"

"None to be had except what you can buy in them eating places, and that is awful expensive. Rather have sarsaparilla anyway," Ted informed him.

"Me too," his brother said.

"Then that makes three of us," Longarm said, digging into his second fish and discovering it was pretty tasty after all.

Chapter 13

When they reached the mercantile, Longarm bought the boys a half pound of hard rock candy and another half pound of licorice. The manager of the store, Mr. Trimble, couldn't stop grinning. "Marshal, them boys sure love candy. Sometimes I give 'em a taste or two if they sweep my floors or carry out some trash."

Longarm was smoking a cheroot and watching the Clum brothers sitting outside on the boardwalk. "They're both good kids and fishermen. What have you got in the way of rifles?"

"You mean like a Winchester for yourself?"

"No, I was thinking of a small rifle or shotgun that the Clum boys can use to hunt squirrel or rabbit."

"They haven't got any money. Not even for the ammunition."

"I'm buying."

Mr. Trimble looked closely at him. "You don't have to do that just because you killed their pa. Harley was no good and you did everyone a favor. He'd hurt quite a few men, and would have gotten stabbed or shot sooner or later even if you never showed your face in these mountains."

"So I've heard. But I asked you a question. What have you got that they could shoot?"

The manager waved a hand at a rifle rack filled with new and used weapons, most of which were high-caliber rifles. "I have nothing for a kid as young as John Clum, but I got a catalogue and I could order 'em something pretty accurate. Might cost you thirty or forty dollars, though."

Longarm counted out a hundred dollars; some of it was from Big Mamma, but most of the cash came right out of his own salary. "I want you to order a quality rifle and plenty of ammunition."

"Marshal, it won't cost *that* much."

"Use the rest to buy them some good shoes and clothes. Nothing fancy, but things that boys in the woods can wear."

Trimble nodded with understanding. "You also have a good heart. And I'll tell you what I'll do. I won't take a dime of profit on any of this merchandise. I'm sure the store's owner will approve. That way, we can get 'em as much as the cost and shipping will allow."

"That is appreciated," Longarm said. "Have you got anything in stock that would fit them today?"

Trimble rubbed his chin and his brow furrowed in thought. "Actually, I do have some pretty nice leather gloves that were ordered by one of the ladies last winter. She got sick and died and I never sold 'em."

"Gloves, huh?"

"That's right. Two pair, and they're made of prime leather with a sheepskin inner lining. They'd come in real handy next winter. I also have a couple of heavy winter jackets that would fit them. They're also leather on the outside to keep out the wet and lined with warm sheep wool. Again, they were ordered by whores . . . I mean women, but who is to know the difference?"

136

"Not me or those boys," Longarm said. "Bring them out and let's see if they fit."

Trimble looked out at the two young kids and said, "They've had it real hard, just like their mother. I once offered Mrs. Clum a job, but she turned it down on account of Harley always coming in here and giving me hell. We didn't like each other. I was scared of him, but too stubborn with pride to back down."

"Why don't you offer her a job again?" Longarm asked. "Maybe without her husband everything would work out fine."

"I believe that I will. But can I ask you something?"

"Sure."

"Who are the Love Sisters and what are they *really* up to?"

"They are planning to help women up in these mining camps."

"Yeah. I heard that. I also have a flyer that they started posting all over town. Marshal, can I be honest with you?"

"Of course."

"Them pretty ladies may mean well, but they're going to stir up a hornet's nest with all this talk of helping women."

"Why is that?"

"There are a lot of men who believe that women ought to work hard, be given all the loving they want, and never complain no matter how tough things get in a marriage."

"I never got the feeling that the Love Sisters want to butt into anyone's family affairs. But what they are concerned with are women and kids like Mrs. Clum and her sons who were beaten, starved, and worked nearly to death."

"That's certainly wrong," Trimble agreed. "But I'm not sure that it's the place of outsiders to interfere."

Longarm disagreed, and tried to make the store manager look at it from his point of view. "Mr. Trimble, if you saw a dog or a horse being beaten unmercifully and for no reason other than the meanness of its owner, wouldn't you want to have a word with that man and advise him that he needed to be civil and decent-acting?"

"I guess I would."

"Then why have less concern for a woman or her kids?"

"You're right," Trimble decided. "I'll not argue because you *are* right. But I'm just saying that the Love Sisters or whatever they call themselves are going to run into a buzz saw. Not only from some husbands who mistreat their wives and kids . . . and I'll admit it happens regularly, and most often on the night of a payday when they get drunk . . . but also from some powerful businessmen."

"Who are you talking about?"

"The owners of the saloons where they hire dance hall girls, and also the two men that own the Speckled Bird and the Calico Cat."

"I'm not worried about them."

"You should be," Trimble insisted. "They are both tough sonsabitches who will fight like hell if they believe the Love Sisters are going to stir up their girls."

"It's a free country. If their 'girls' want to come to the meeting, then they should have the right to do so."

"Jake Garwood and Adam Salter won't let their girls out of their places, and I expect the same can be said of the saloon girls who also work in little back rooms for what they can earn spreading their legs."

"I can't change the ways things are. If those women can't get to the meeting, I suppose there's not much that can be done."

Trimble leaned closer. "Marshal, Jake Garwood and Adam Salter run this town. They have the money and we need their money to stay in business. So what I'm telling you is confidential. Understand?"

"Sure, and I appreciate the warning."

138

"Those men play rough. They won't tolerate agitators in Oreville. Not even high-minded ladies like you brought in on the stage. So all I'm saying is that you need to watch them ladies real careful or they could have sudden accidents."

"I follow your meaning. Now, how about a look at those gloves and coats. And for hell sakes, don't mention they were ordered by whores."

"I won't. And, if the boys like them . . . I'll also give them to you at cost."

"You have a heart of gold, Mr. Trimble."

When John and Ted saw the gloves and coats, and were asked if they fit and would they like to have them for their own, the brothers couldn't believe their ears.

"You mean," John stammered, "you'd *give* them to us?"

"Yep," Longarm said, feeling good inside. "Mr. Trimble and I want you to have them . . . if they fit and you like 'em."

"Oh," Ted whispered, "they're gonna fit fine!"

The boys donned their coats in a flash, buttoning them up all the way to their necks and then running over to a mirror to admire themselves.

"What do you think?" Longarm asked, the answer already splashed across their smiling faces. "Will the new coats do?"

"Yes, sir!" both boys said in unison.

"Then try on the gloves."

The gloves turned out to be small for both boys, but Longarm soothed their disappointment by promising to order bigger pairs. "And in the meantime, Mr. Trimble is going to measure you both up for some new shirts, pants, and shoes."

"Gosh!" Ted exclaimed. "And this ain't even Christmas!"

"It is for us," his brother proclaimed, grinning from ear to ear.

It took some doing to get the boys out of the mercantile. Their next visit was at the barbershop, where they all had haircuts and Longarm enjoyed a smooth shave.

"You lookin' after the Clum boys, huh?" the barber, a potbellied man with a good-natured smile and balding gray hair, observed.

"I suppose I am."

"It's good to see 'em finally get a little attention. Harley would come in here and get a haircut and shave. But he never brought the boys. Their mother must have cut their hair with dull scissors. That family never had anything but hard times."

"I think their lives will improve now."

"Oh?" The barber's eyebrows raised in question.

"Yes," Longarm said. "Wouldn't surprise me if Mrs. Clum got remarried someday to a better man."

"There's plenty around who'd like to wed the woman. She's still pretty good-looking. She just needs to fatten up a mite. Hell, if I were twenty years younger and single, I'd give that little lady a second and then even a third look. She's a worker and a good woman. I'm just worried about what she's buyin' into with them Love Sisters."

"A better life."

"I hope so, but you might be surprised. Could turn sour quick."

"You mean because of Mr. Garwood and Mr. Salter?"

"Marshal, I didn't say that."

"But that's what you meant, isn't it?"

"I'm just saying that people don't like things stirred up. They like things orderly and predictable. I do myself. Now, them pretty ladies you brought into town are gonna agitate everyone, and that isn't good. Could even be unhealthy."

The boys had gone outside to play, and Longarm was

the barber's only customer, so he said, "You're trying to warn me. Maybe you're even saying it would be healthier if we all climbed back on the stagecoach and left Oreville."

"Marshal, I'm just tellin' you to be careful and to watch out for them ladies. Especially at the town meeting they've called for tonight."

"Tonight?"

"Yep. Didn't you hear?"

"No."

"Well, the news is out that it'll be held at the west end of the street."

"I thought they were having it at the church."

"Nope," the barber said. "The Reverend Jacob Haskell said there was no room for politics and unholiness in the house of the Lord."

Longarm's jaw tightened until the muscles in his cheeks stood out. "I don't see that trying to help women like Mrs. Clum is contrary to God's plan."

"The Reverend Jacob Haskell sure does. I guess he and that great big woman almost got into a fistfight. About ten o'clock this morning, you could hear them yelling at each other all the way through town. I heard that the big woman chased Reverend Haskell right into his church and gave him hell!"

The barber chuckled. "I'd have given all I own to have seen that skinny hypocrite chased into his church! But you can be sure that there will be a lot of people who won't find it nearly so humorous."

"I don't find it a bit humorous," Longarm told the man. "I think it's pathetic that someone who ought to be standing up for what is moral and right takes that kind of position."

"Just be careful. Mr. Garwood and Mr. Salter own a couple of saloons in this town as well as the whorehouses. If some of their girls start thinking that they deserve a

141

better life, then you can expect them to send trouble your way."

"You mean they wouldn't do their own dirty work?"

"Why should they when they both hire thugs and bullies?"

"Maybe," Longarm said, "I ought to go by and introduce myself to that pair before tonight's meeting."

"They wouldn't be pleased to make your acquaintance."

"Good. Where can I find them?"

"Speckled Bird is owned by Adam Salter. Jake Garwood owns the Calico Cat. You'd think they were competitors, but they aren't. I have a feeling that they are partners. They swap girls and keep the prices up for their services. Now and then a new gal will come into Oreville and try to make a little quick money up in her hotel room. She'll be real independent. You know what I mean?"

"Sure. And I expect that Salter and Garwood would not approve of the competition to their girls."

"That's the truth. Why, the last one that stopped over to make some quick money on the mattress wound up losing her front teeth. She left here in the back of a buckboard beaten half to death."

"Garwood and Salter?"

"No. They sent a couple men over to deliver the message. After the pair used the woman up in her room all in one afternoon, they beat her senseless and hauled her naked down to the street, where they threw her in a buckboard. You can bet that the word went out far and wide to any other prostitutes in Colorado that they better steer way clear of Oreville."

"Subtle, huh? Who are the two men that beat the woman?"

"Couple of bruisers named Max and Otto. Big men like yourself. When people see them coming down the boardwalk, they step aside or they get knocked on their ass. Max and Otto are twin brothers. They have shaved heads and look like a pair of ugly bookends. I wouldn't want to see you have to try and arrest them boys."

"Who do they work for?"

"Max works at the Calico Cat, and Otto works at the Speckled Bird."

Longarm closed his eyes and let the barber finish his shave. The blade was sharp, and trouble awaited.

"Be two dollars for three haircuts and a shave."

Longarm paid the man. "Thanks for the names and warning."

"Maybe you should tell them ladies not to have their meeting tonight," the barber said in a low, confidential voice. "I think it very unwise."

Longarm pulled on his coat and set his snuff-brown hat down just right on his head. "You could be right, but this is a free country. Those ladies have a right to hold their meeting. And other women have a right to attend. It's one of the rights we have in this country which I am sworn to uphold."

"Be careful if you go to the Speckled Bird or the Calico Cat. You got a clean-shaven face and a handsome mug. Be a shame to see it all messed up so soon."

Longarm spent another hour with the Clum boys, then figured it was time to send them home. "I had a good time fishing," he said in all sincerity.

"Even though you didn't catch anything?" John asked.

"Sure. But I got to eat some fish, didn't I?"

"You did," John replied. "Wanna go fishing again tomorrow morning?"

"I better wait and see how things are going here in town."

"You mean on account of that meeting tonight?"

"Yes," Longarm admitted. "You saw the flyers, huh?"

"Couldn't hardly miss them," Ted replied. "They was posted all over town. Is my mother coming tonight?"

"It wouldn't surprise me."

Both boys suddenly looked worried.

"It'll be all right," Longarm promised.

"You don't know this town, mister. We overheard some men talking, and they said that there would be hell to pay tonight and that the Love Sisters might even be tarred and feathered."

"That won't happen." Longarm knelt on one knee and looked both boys in the eye before he said, "I'm a United States marshal and it's my job to uphold the law. I won't allow anyone to bully or beat those ladies or anyone else who comes to hear what they have to say."

"I hope not," John said, still looking upset. "And no offense, Marshal Long, but you're only one man."

"That's true, but I have the law on my side."

"Will the law stand up against a bullet?" Ted whispered as he nervously wrung his hands.

Longarm took a deep breath. "I just know what I have to do and that is protect the rights of people to speak their piece. Now, if something bad was to happen to me . . . that would only bring more lawmen. No one is above the law, though a lot of men think they are."

"Like our father," John said.

"Yes, and those other two. They all knew what they did was not only wrong but a crime. But they didn't care, and the law came back and made them pay with their lives."

"We're more worried about Mom and you than the law."

"Of course you are." Longarm stuck out his hand and said, "I'm giving you my word that your mother will come to no harm. And neither will I."

"You already got a bad knee and a bad butt."

"How'd you know about the butt?" Longarm asked with surprise.

"We could tell. You walk a little funny."

"I'll have to work on that," Longarm said with a grin. "Now get on home and I'll see you tomorrow."

"You promise?" Ted asked, pulling his fine new coat tighter around his slim body.

"I promise."

The boys left then, and Longarm headed for the Speckled Bird and the Calico Cat. He wasn't looking forward to meeting Otto or Max or Jake Garwood or Adam Salter, but better now than after they did something that would send them all to prison.

Chapter 14

Longarm chanced upon the Calico Cat first. Making sure that his badge was hidden from view, he stepped inside, entering a luxurious parlor with expensive red velvet chairs ringing most of its perimeter. Heavy curtains blocked out the sunlight, and an impressive crystal chandelier hung overhead, supplying a dim, flickering light. There was a glistening mahogany bar directly across the room, and behind it stood a large, muscle-bound, and bald-headed man in a formal suit and tie. This, Longarm remembered from his conversation with the barber, was Max.

Max smiled without warmth and said in a surprisingly soft, ingratiating voice, "Good afternoon. Would you like a drink on the house before you meet the girls?"

"Sure. Whiskey, if it's of quality."

"*Everything* here is quality," the man promised. "Especially our ladies."

"Is that right?"

"Don't take my word for it," Max said, handing Longarm a shot glass filled to the brim. "Taste the drink and the women and tell me I'm wrong."

Longarm returned the man's thin smile, raised the glass to his lips, and sampled a taste.

"Well?" Max asked. "Was I wrong?"

"Yes, you were wrong, but not about this whiskey."

The man's smile slipped noticeably. His lips drew down at the corners. "What is that supposed to mean?"

"It means I heard about that woman that you and your brother beat half to death before dumping her in a buckboard and sending her down the line."

"What are you talking about?" Max asked, no longer smiling at all.

"The whore that you and your brother used before knocking out her teeth." With his left hand, Longarm raised his half-filled glass of whiskey and said, "Now *that* was very wrong."

Max turned nasty. "Who the hell do—"

Longarm hurled the remaining whiskey into Max's brutish face. Before the man could clear his burning eyes, Longarm grabbed both of his ears and slammed his face down on the edge of the heavy bar. Max gasped with pain and tried to rear back, but Longarm jumped up, hooked his right elbow behind the man's head, and slammed his face down on the bar once more, using every ounce of his considerable weight and strength. The heavy bar shook, glasses danced on polished wood, and Max hung on the edge of the bar as if impaled by invisible hooks.

When Longarm released the thug, Max finally staggered backward, his nose smashed to pulp by the first blow, all his front teeth broken and his lips a crimson pulp due to the second blow. The man gripped the bar with one hand to steady himself, then reached low to find what Longarm was certain was a gun.

"A little slow there, Max." Longarm drew his six-gun and laid a deep crease across the crown of Max's bald head, sending him down for the rest of the afternoon.

"I just hate a man who beats up women and kids," Longarm said, looking over the bar and then pouring himself a refill . . . on the house.

"Who are you!" a scantily dressed woman demanded.

Longarm tossed down his whiskey, turned to the anxious woman, and said, "I'm United States Deputy Marshal Custis Long, at your service."

She was several years past her prime and plump, with black hair and so much face powder that she reminded Longarm of a bloated cadaver. "I've come to see your boss, Mr. Jake Garwood."

"He don't want to see you."

"Too bad."

Longarm placed his glass down carefully and folded his arms. The woman, meanwhile, went around behind the bar, and Longarm heard her take a sharp intake of breath. She was obviously shocked, and that was impressive since Longarm was certain the woman had seen everything base and violent at one time or another.

Then she turned her attention back to Longarm. "You really hurt him bad."

"Like he and his brother hurt the woman they pitched into the back of a wagon? Or maybe like he's hurt you or one of the other girls who work here?"

Longarm saw her blink, and he knew he'd hit a nerve. She took a deep breath. "You better leave right now, Marshal."

"Why? Is Otto here? Or is Mr. Garwood going to lay into me with both fists?"

"Oh, hell," the woman said, "if you could do that to Max, you can probably whip both Otto and Mr. Garwood at the same time."

"Where is he?"

"In his office with someone."

"Man . . . or woman?"

"A woman who needs a job real bad . . . or should I say a real bad job?"

"He's . . . interviewing?"

148

"Yeah." She almost smiled. "It'd be a real poor time to disturb the boss, don't you see."

"Of course. Now, do you want to lead the way, or should I start yanking open doors until I find him?"

"Jeezus, Marshal, you are bound for hell or glory, ain't you?"

"What's your name?"

"Alma."

"Lead the way."

"Marshal, before we do this, do you mind if I see your badge first?"

Longarm showed it to her. "Hmmm. Big man. Big badge. Come along."

With his bad knee beginning to throb, Custis limped down a hallway lit by candles and filled with the aroma of incense. When Alma came to the last door, she paused and said, "This is where I'm leaving."

"Thanks." Longarm knocked on the door.

"Get lost, gawdammit!" a man shouted in a hoarse voice. "I'm busy!"

Longarm turned the handle, but it was locked. So he stepped back and kicked the door, splintering wood and knocking it completely off its hinges. He looked inside to see Jake Garwood with his pants down being attended to by a naked young woman on her knees.

Garwood was about six feet tall with brown hair, thin arms, a sunken chest, and a round little paunch. He was still wearing a pair of black socks. Now, he tried to free himself from the woman, but she had her arms wrapped around his bare thighs and would not let go.

"My name is Marshal Custis Long," Longarm said as naturally as if he had met the brothel owner on the street. "I understand that you are opposed to the meeting that is to be held by the Love Sisters tonight. Is that correct?"

Garwood's jaw drooped. "What . . . are you crazy?"

"Not crazy. Just concerned that you or Mr. Salter might

149

take it upon yourselves to do something stupid and unlawful. Because if you did, I'd have to arrest you both and that would be the end of these . . . interviews. You wouldn't like that, would you?"

"Dammit! I'll have you . . . Max!"

"He's sorta under the weather," Longarm explained. He looked down at the young woman, who had scurried off to hide her nakedness behind a chair. "Are you sure you want to work here? My advice, young lady, would be to attend tonight's meeting instead. Could be you can do a whole lot better standing tall than . . . well, doing what you were just doing to that snake."

"Get out of here!" Garwood commanded. "You have no right to come into my place of business, damage property, and insult us!"

But instead of retreating back into the hallway, Longarm entered the man's office and looked around. In contrast to the parlor, this room was seedy. The desk was old and scarred, the furniture shabby, except for a bed, which left little doubt that Jake Garwood spent a good deal of his time in the prone position with his girls.

"I'm warning you," Longarm told the man, his voice turning cold. "If you or any one of your people attempt to disrupt tonight's meeting, I'll come back here and make you wish you'd never been born."

"I'm . . . I'm a legitimate businessman! You can't threaten me."

"I don't ever threaten. I just give a warning, and if you don't pay attention to it, then you'll have no one to blame but yourself. And as for being a legitimate businessman, you're lower than a snake's belly. You're slime."

Garwood spluttered, but he looked so ridiculous with his stiff manhood beginning to droop that it was all Longarm could do to keep from laughing.

When he limped back out to the parlor, Alma was standing at the bar with two of the house girls. "See," she

150

said, "I told you he was big and handsome."

"You weren't lying this time," a red-haired woman said, eyeing Longarm from head to toe. "Say, mister, maybe you could come back sometime."

"Not very damn likely," he replied. "But thanks for the invitation. Why don't you women come to the meeting tonight?"

"And lose our jobs?"

"Not much to lose, if you ask me," Longarm replied, tipping his hat to the three of them and then heading outside.

The Speckled Bird was across the street, and Longarm could see before he reached the front door that this was a lower-class brothel. The outside was unpainted, and when he stepped through the doorway, instead of luxury, he saw a no-nonsense room with worn couches and a bar that consisted of a wooden plank laid across two empty whiskey barrels. A few of the painted ladies were drinking with men in preparation for more intimate surroundings. When the other women saw Longarm, they smiled and two of them came to introduce themselves.

"I'm Trudy," a busty brunette said, flapping her eyelashes and giving Longarm a smile.

"And I'm Opal," said the other as she slipped her arm around Longarm's waist. "You got a favorite . . . or would you like to have a taste of us both?"

Trudy's laugh was coarse and loud. Longarm was repelled by both women, and extracted himself from Opal's grasp, then said, "I'm here to see Mr. Salter."

"He can't do what I can do for you," Trudy cooed.

"Men," Opal said, "don't come here looking for men. They come here looking for a good time with a lady."

Longarm was tempted to say that they were not, by any definition of the word, ladies. But instead he replied, "Where is Mr. Salter?"

"He's off somewhere," Opal replied. "Who cares?"

"I do." Longarm surveyed the room. "Ladies," he said in a loud voice, "I am United States Deputy Marshal Custis Long. And I'm here to say that you are all invited to a street meeting tonight that could change your lives for the better."

"You mean one that will get us *fired*," Trudy shouted.

"This is no life," Longarm answered. "What woman among you doesn't know that it'll take you to the gutter?"

"Hey!" a miner bellowed, pushing a girl off his lap and coming at Longarm with blood in his eye. "These women don't need nobody telling them what they can or can't do. You ain't no preacher, so don't be spouting off any more of that righteous bullshit!"

"Go back and sit down," Longarm told the man as he caught sight of Otto, Max's twin brother. Unlike his brother, Otto was dressed in a workingman's clothes and his muscular forearms were folded across his broad chest. For the moment, at least, he seemed content to let one of the customers test Longarm's abilities.

"Why don't you get out of here," the miner said, breathing whiskey fumes in Longarm's face.

"Go back and sit down," Longarm ordered.

"Not until I toss your ass out the door," the man hissed, balling his fists and then throwing a roundhouse punch aimed for Longarm's jaw.

Custis ducked and hammered a tremendous uppercut to the man's belly, which landed just under his sternum. The customer's mouth flew open, his eyes bulged, and he doubled up, clutching his belly and fighting for air.

Longarm's eyes traveled across the room. "Otto," he said, "I suggest you help this man outside before he gets sick and throws up your bad whiskey in his gut."

"What do you want?" the bouncer graveled.

"I want you to tell Adam Salter that I'll be watching for him . . . and you . . . tonight at the meeting. If I see either of you there . . . you'll be arrested."

"Big talk."

Longarm glanced down at the man on his knees still struggling to breathe. "I can back up my talk . . . if I have to. If you don't believe me, ask your brother when he finally regains consciousness and tries to talk with a mouth full of broken teeth."

Otto's close-set eyes narrowed with suspicion. "You been over to the Calico Cat?"

"That's right. They weren't happy to see me either. Especially poor Max."

Otto sneered and he started across the room, then pulled up short when Longarm's hand came to rest on the butt of his six-gun. "I don't believe you," Otto said.

"That could be a fatal mistake."

Otto advanced several more steps, so Longarm drew his pistol and said, "Stop right where you are."

"You won't gun me down in cold blood if you really are a marshal."

"Oh, I'm a sworn officer of the law, all right," Longarm told the man as he flashed his badge. "So you'd better listen to me when I tell you to stay clear of the Love Sisters. And tell your boss to do the same. Otherwise, you'll wind up looking like your poor, dumb brother."

Pure hatred radiated from Otto's black eyes. He turned and disappeared, probably heading out the back door on his way over to the Calico Cat. Longarm could only imagine the man's reaction when he found poor Max looking as if he'd stepped in front of a runaway wagon.

"You're all invited to attend the meeting tonight, ladies."

One of the least attractive of the women said, "What can them fancy ladies do to help us?"

"I don't know. You'll have to let them tell you."

"They can't do nothing but get us fired!" a tall, angular woman wearing a soiled green silk dress and fake jewels snapped with defiance. She lit a cigar, jammed it between her teeth, and hissed, "Mary Jane Riley don't need no help from no one!"

Longarm had no intention of arguing with Mary Jane Riley, so he turned and limped back outside, then headed for his room to take a nap. He'd given his fair warning. Now, it was up to Garwood, Salter, and any other of Oreville's woman-abusing sonsabitches if they wanted to pay heed.

Chapter 15

Despite his warning to both Jake Garwood and Adam Salter, Longarm was still expecting trouble that evening. It must have showed, because Big Mamma said, "How come you look so grim?"

"Do I?"

"Yes."

He forced a smile. "I hope everything goes all right this evening and that neither you or any of the Love Sisters get hurt."

"You'll be there ready to protect us, won't you?"

"Sure. But I can't watch everyone. Georgia, if there's a crowd of drunk and angry hecklers, I can't guarantee anyone's safety."

"We know that. It's something we've already discussed and we are prepared to accept as a risk."

"All right," Longarm told her. "I'm going to take a look around town, and if I see anyone drunk and threatening to raise hell when you ladies appear, I'll take care of them before they can cause trouble."

"I heard what you did to Max over at the Calico Cat. You don't go to any pains in order to avoid trouble, do you?"

Longarm shook his head. "In my experience, it's best to head trouble off quick. I wanted Garwood and Salter to know that I mean business."

"I hear you really hurt Garwood's bodyguard and bouncer."

"He deserved it."

Big Mamma came over and put her arms around Longarm's neck. "I'm more worried about someone ambushing or stabbing you in the dark than I am about us. Just watch your backside, Custis."

Longarm went outside. The sun was just setting in the west, and the air temperature was falling fast. Dark clouds were building toward the north, and the wind was starting to pick up. As he crossed the street, Longarm decided that a storm was coming in later that night.

"Hey, Marshal!"

Longarm whirled, hand moving toward his gun.

"Whoa," a slender, well-dressed young man said, raising both hands to show that he was unarmed. "I'm on *your* side."

"What is that supposed to mean?" Longarm asked, relaxing.

"Just that I don't want to see the Love Sisters hurt any more than you do." The stranger smiled disarmingly. "I met one of them in the mercantile today and we really hit it off, if you know what I mean."

"No," Longarm said, trying to figure the man out. "I don't."

"She told me her name is Miss Elizabeth Hanson. She has reddish-brown hair and a smile that would even melt the heart of a barbarian. We talked, and I told her that I'd like to see her again. Maybe take her for a walk in the moonlight after tonight's meeting."

"I don't think that would be a very good idea."

The man's engaging smile slipped. "Why? Is she married?"

"No."

The smile reappeared. "Well, Marshal, you're certainly not old enough to be her father ... are you her big brother?"

"Of course not."

"Then what is the problem? Last I heard, this was a free country, and Elizabeth appears old enough to make her own decisions."

Longarm hooked his thumbs in his cartridge belt. "Look," he began, "I can't order you to stay away from Elizabeth. But I can tell you that she and the other Love Sisters come from a different world."

"What does that mean?"

"The young lady has wealth in her family. She's from the East and she's returning to the East when this is finished."

"So what? I'm not proposing marriage to the girl. I'd just like to see her again. My name is Peter Bradley and I own the only mercantile in Oreville. I'm not rich ... but I do very well financially and have plans to do even better in the future. I assure you that I'm not after Elizabeth or her money."

Longarm believed the man. "Look, Pete, I didn't mean to come on hard. And I appreciate your intentions. But there is trouble brewing in this town and I'm concerned about those ladies."

"So am I." Bradley frowned. "I've heard the talk, and some of it is getting pretty nasty. That's the other part of why I wanted to talk to you. Maybe you could use a little help."

"Of course I could."

"Then I'm here to offer my services."

"No offense, but you aren't even packing a gun."

"Actually, I am," Peter admitted, opening his suit coat so that Longarm could see that he wore a shoulder holster and pistol. "Sorry about the lie."

"That's all right. I can usually spot those, but your rig is expertly fitted. Can you use that gun?"

"I'm an excellent shot."

"Let's hope there isn't any trouble," Longarm told the man. "And the reason that I tried to discourage you from taking Miss Elizabeth for a walk in the moonlight isn't because I want to play her father . . . it's because I am charged with being her protector. If you took Elizabeth for a moonlight stroll and someone jumped you and hurt or even killed her . . . I'd be responsible."

"I can take care of myself," Bradley said, a little defensively. "The people in this town know and respect my abilities. I assure you that I'd never put the young woman's life in any danger."

"Fine," Longarm told the man. "You don't need my permission, but you have it anyway. If Elizabeth wants to go with you for a walk after the meeting, just be very careful."

"Your advice is both heard and accepted." Bradley started to leave, but then changed his mind and said, "My family lives in Baltimore. My father was a United States Congressman and his father owned one of the largest newspapers in the state of Maryland. So, for your information, there is also money in my family."

"Then what are you doing running a mercantile in Oreville?"

"I came West seeking adventure and found it. Then, I fell in love with these mountains and decided I needed to figure out a way to make my own good fortune. So I bought the mercantile and have doubled both its size and annual sales. In a year or two I mean to open up a second, much larger store in Cripple Creek."

"Sounds like an excellent plan."

"I'll be successful." Bradley shrugged. "Marshal Long, you're only a couple of years older than myself. Don't you ever weary of working for small wages and then dream of making your own fortune?"

"No," Longarm replied without a shred of guilt for lacking Bradley's ambition. "I make a decent living and I do what I enjoy."

Bradley looked up and down the street. A crowd had already gathered at the south end of the town where tonight's meeting was to be held. "You mean to tell me that you actually *like* this kind of trouble?"

"No," Longarm confessed, "I don't. But someone has to do it and I'm very good at the job. If there is to be a ruckus or a riot over what the Love Sisters tell the women of Oreville, I feel that I am as well qualified as anyone to diffuse the situation."

"Well," Bradley said, looking genuinely puzzled, "I can't understand what would possess a man to enjoy this kind of situation, but I promise to be available if you need any assistance."

"That's nice to know," Longarm said, extending his hand. "And I hope you enjoy your walk with Miss Hanson later this evening in the moonlight."

"I will," Bradley assured him as he left.

Longarm pinned on his lawman's tin star, then strolled casually down the street to the gathering crowd of miners and other workingmen. "Evening, gents," he said in as friendly a voice as he could muster.

When they saw him and the badge, several of the men left the group and hurried off, probably to drink more liquor. Most, however, stood rooted in the middle of the street. One of them said, "Is this where them meddlin' Love Sisters are supposed to have their meeting?"

"I believe so. But the meeting is for women." Longarm looked the men over, his eyes turning hard. "So what are you boys here for?"

No one would answer him.

"We're just getting some fresh air," one of the men

finally said as he rolled a cigarette and then shoved it between his lips. "No law against that, is there, Marshal?"

"None at all." Longarm knew this was the time to be firm and show his authority. "But when this meeting starts, I want all of you to go back inside."

"Now wait a minute here," another man protested. "I might like to hear what them so-called Love Sisters have to say. No harm in that, is there?"

Before Longarm could reply, another blustered, "Of course there ain't. This is still a free country, ain't it?"

"Yeah," Custis replied, turning on the man. "And the Love Sisters have a right to say what they want."

"And we have a right to say what we want right back," the man growled with his cigarette dangling from his lips.

The others nodded in agreement, and Longarm could feel their rising hostility. "Boys," he said, "you can go back inside the saloon right now, or head on up the street and take your fresh air someplace else. It doesn't matter to me."

"What," the man with the smoking cigarette hissed, "if we don't want to move on or go back inside?"

"That's easy," Longarm said, fixing his eyes on the man. "If you don't do as I say, I'll arrest you."

"Hellfire, Marshal, there ain't even a damn jail in this town."

Longarm's hands moved fast. One moment he was giving the man fair warning; the next he had him spun completely around with one arm bent up behind his back and stepping up Main Street.

"You can't arrest me for no reason!" the man bellowed, grunting with pain.

Longarm bent his arm even higher until his prisoner was walking on his toes and moaning. A crowd watched as Longarm found a tree, then shoved his prisoner up against it and said, "Hug that tree. If you move, I'll figure that you are trying to escape and I'll shoot you in the leg."

"You're crazy!"

"Maybe, but you'd better not test me again or you'll walk with a limp the rest of your life."

The man spat out his cigarette, wrapped his arms around the tree, and hugged it like it was his best girl or his dear mother. Longarm went over to a saddle horse tied at the nearest hitching rail and removed a lariat from the saddle. He returned and bound his prisoner to the tree.

"Now," he said, "you can breathe all the fresh air you want."

"Dammit, you can't do this to me!"

"I did it and I'll do worse to anyone else who plans on opposing me." He glared at the watchful crowd of angry, muttering men. "Everyone inside or else get out of town!"

The men turned and walked stiffly back into the saloons. Longarm could hear them cursing him, but he didn't care. The streets were cleared and the meeting was about to begin. He'd done the right thing, even if he had sort of robbed the men of their right to free assembly.

The Love Sisters, with Big Mamma in the lead, took chairs that had been placed in the middle of the street, and then sat and waited to see if any of the Oreville women would dare to appear. The north wind rose higher and dust began to blow into their faces. Nothing was said, but the wind's deepening moan could be heard moving through the nearby pines. A street sign banged noisily against a wall someplace, and everyone heard the ominous rumble of approaching thunder. But not one Oreville woman appeared, and the last light from a dying sun faded like the hopes of the Love Sisters.

Longarm couldn't help but feel a mixture of relief . . . but also disappointment. Relief because he'd thought the whole idea of helping mining women must inevitably fail. To his way of thinking they were victims of an age and

161

circumstances beyond anyone's control. Frontier life was hard and often cruel. But he also felt a keen and undeniable disappointment because, when he thought of women like Mrs. Clum and so many others that he'd seen subjected to treatment not suited for a dog, he hoped for a permanent change for the better.

Back in the center of the street, Big Mamma finally glanced down the line of seated Love Sisters, and started to say something just as Mrs. Clum and three other women appeared from the shadows. Longarm saw Big Mamma's face break into a wide smile, and the Love Sisters leaped from their seats to embrace Mrs. Clum and her brave friends.

"Thank you for coming!" Big Mamma shouted in a voice that carried the entire length of that little mining town. She turned to look up the street, and her eyes came to rest on Custis. He saw her smile, then say in a voice that shook with righteous conviction, "This evening may prove to be historic and we hope to take measures to better the lives of mining women forever."

Longarm leaned back against a porch post, eyes constantly scanning up and down the street as he watched for trouble.

"We believe that women have the right to live decently and with dignity," Big Mamma continued. "We are all children of God and—"

She didn't have a chance to finish because, suddenly, a rifle boomed and she was struck in the chest. Women screamed as Big Mamma collapsed in the street, blood pumping from her chest.

Longarm's gun was already in his fist as he twisted around seeking the hidden assassin. But any telltale puff of smoke that might have pinpointed the shooter's location was whisked away by the wind, and he spotted absolutely nothing.

"Where did the shot come from?" he shouted, frantically looking up at rooftops. "Did anyone see a muzzle blast?"

The Love Sisters were crowded around Big Mamma, and their cries of anguish could be heard over the mournful keening of the wind. Rage filled Longarm as he ran over to the fallen woman's side and knelt in the dirt knowing that Georgia—or Big Mamma as she was called by her pretty and rich Eastern girls—was already dead.

Another shot shattered the night, and Elizabeth Hanson screamed as a slug spun her halfway around. From out of nowhere, Peter Bradley appeared, firing his gun up at a rooftop.

"Where is he?" Longarm shouted, jumping up and spinning around.

"He was on my roof!" Bradley yelled.

"Stay here and protect them!" Longarm ordered as he took off running up the street. There was an alley behind Bradley's mercantile and, if he got lucky, he'd be able to intercept the deadly assassin on his way down to the back alley, which was his most likely escape.

Chapter 16

Because of his bum knee, Longarm wasn't able to move with anything near his normal speed. But even so, it took him no more than a few minutes to round the far corner of Bradley's mercantile and come to a skidding halt in the dark alley. His heart was pounding so loudly, and so many people were out in the street shouting and raising a ruckus, that he could not hear a thing. Moving slowly forward in almost complete darkness, Longarm strained to listen, and when he heard the sound of running feet, he jumped forward and collided with an empty rain barrel. His bad knee struck the ground hard, and he roared in pain and frustration as he crawled back to his feet.

By the time he was on his feet again and hobbling forward, the assassin had vanished. Cussing his bad luck, Longarm returned to the main street, hoping to see the killer emerge from the alley and make an attempt to rejoin the crowd. But that didn't happen.

Longarm hobbled back to Big Mamma and the Love Sisters. Elizabeth had already been carried off the street and into the nearest saloon, where she'd been placed on a bar top. Longarm had to fight his way through a mob in order to reach her side.

"How is she?" he asked Peter Bradley.

"I'm afraid she might be dying," the man said, eyes bleak with hopelessness.

Longarm took Elizabeth's wrist and felt a weak, fluttering pulse. He made a quick examination of the wound, and determined that the rifle slug had entered her side and that the young woman had lost a great deal of blood. Looking up, he asked, "Is there a doctor in Oreville?"

"No."

"A dentist?"

"I'm sorry. There isn't anyone here. The nearest professional lives in Gold Creek and—"

Alice Fairchild was standing beside Elizabeth, and interrupted to say, "My uncle was a doctor and I've watched him do surgery. Marshal, if there's any hope at all of saving Elizabeth, I'll assist you in any way that I can."

"So will I," Milly vowed with a voice that trembled.

But Longarm turned to the young merchant. "Bradley?"

"Yeah?"

"Clear this saloon. We're going to try and dig out that bullet."

Bradley went right to work, and Longarm ripped Elizabeth's dress open to expose the ugly wound. The bullet hole was seeping dark blood, and he rolled up his shirtsleeves, then reached for his pocketknife.

"You're going to use *that* to cut her open?" Milly asked, looking horrified.

"I am unless you have a better knife."

"As a matter of fact, I do," Milly said, reaching into her purse and extracting a long, slender knife. "I carry it for protection. It's very sharp."

Longarm opened it, and then tested the sharpness of the steel. It was sharp, and the blade might even be long enough to dig out the bullet. "Whiskey," he ordered.

Alice gave him a bottle and Longarm took a long drink, then splashed some of the liquor on Elizabeth's side and some on the knife, just as he'd seen many a frontier doctor do before surgery. "Here goes," he said, gritting his teeth and easing the point of Milly's knife blade into the bullet hole.

This was not the first bullet that Longarm had been forced to remove, and it probably would not be the last. He'd had lead dug out of his own body on several occasions, and he wasn't tentative or squeamish as he began to cut deeply into Elizabeth's soft, pale flesh.

"Oh, my God," Alice breathed, gripping the edge of the bar and then grabbing the bottle of whiskey and taking a long, shuddering pull. "I hope you know what you are doing."

"I don't," Longarm admitted. "All I'm sure of is that I have to get the slug out or it will fester and Elizabeth will sicken, then die of lead poisoning."

Elizabeth groaned and thrashed as Longarm probed even deeper. Peter Bradley pinned her arms to her side so that she didn't accidentally strike Longarm's hand and perhaps cause unnecessary injury.

"Do you feel anything like lead?" Bradley asked, looking badly shaken but determined to keep Elizabeth still.

"Not yet. I have to go still deeper."

Milly grabbed the bottle and took a couple of rough swallows. "I can't believe what a nightmare this has become. Big Mamma dead. Elizabeth—"

"Shhh!" Alice commanded. "We can cry and mourn later. Right now, we need a miracle and lots of prayer and courage."

"You're right," Milly said as she closed her eyes and began to pray.

Longarm was forced to make an even larger surface incision, which caused more hemorrhaging. He hated that, but knew that every minute was precious and that the sooner he could get that slug, the sooner he could close the wound and then worry about how to suture it.

"Bradley?"

"Yeah."

"If we're lucky, we'll need a needle and thread to sew her up. Can you find any?"

"You bet I can!"

Bradley raced out the front door. By now, the crowd knew what was taking place, and dozens of faces were pressed against the saloon's dirty front window. It seemed like the whole town was holding its breath as Longarm finally located the twisted metal and eased it out of the wound, using the blade and his forefinger.

"Here," Alice said, handing him a clean bar towel. "It's the best we can do."

Longarm pressed the bar towel hard against Elizabeth's side. It was immediately saturated with blood, and he called for more towels. Minutes later, a badly winded Peter Bradley appeared with a needle and some thick black thread.

"Forgive me but I can hardly stand to watch this," he said, looking pale as he held on to the edge of the bar.

Custis had big hands that were ill-suited for the delicate stitching. He looked at Alice. "Is her heart still beating?"

Alice took the pulse. "Yes!"

Longarm splashed some whiskey on the wound and wiped it clean, but the bleeding continued. "Then I'd appreciate it if you or Milly would do the patch-up work. I'm not good with needles and thread."

"I'm not either," Alice told him. "I'm never sewed anything in my life."

"I have," Milly told them. She took another shuddering slug from the bottle and said in a firm voice, "Give me the needle and thread and I'll do it."

Milly threaded the needle, hands as steady as a blacksmith's anvil. She took a deep breath, then expertly sutured the wound in a quarter of the time it would have taken Longarm. As soon as that was finished, Alice pressed more bar towels down over the torn flesh, and Bradley offered his belt to hold them in place.

"Her color is really bad," Alice whispered. "But her heart won't quit. I think Elizabeth has a chance now."

"So do I," Milly agreed. "But poor Big Mamma."

"Her name was Georgia O'Grady," Longarm corrected, wiping the blood from his hands and rolling down his sleeves. "I think that she would have liked us to call her that instead."

"You're right," Alice replied. "She was big and tough on the outside, but had a loving heart. Most of all, she believed in us and what we were trying to do."

Milly swallowed and choked back tears. "Marshal, you should have seen her with Mrs. Clum. She was wonderful. Alice, Elizabeth, and I just watched in awe as she talked to that poor woman and made her think that her life really could improve and that her boys would be far better off without that horrible husband you killed."

"Georgia was a good woman, all right," Longarm agreed. "We'll give her a fine burial."

Longarm went outside. The crowd was larger than ever, and he felt white-hot anger rise up in his throat when he saw the canvas shroud that covered Georgia's body.

"We're real sorry about this," a miner said with his hat in his hand and tears spilling from his eyes. "We talked bad about them Love Sisters but . . . honest to gawd, Marshal, we wouldn't have hurt 'em for the world!"

Longarm studied the man's face. He saw genuine grief, which was reflected in the faces of the others. "Well," he said, "it's done and nothing we can do or say will bring the lady back."

"We're gonna pass the hat and give her a burial like nobody has ever had in Oreville!" someone pledged.

"That's right!" another shouted. "Let's all pass the hat!"

Longarm appreciated the gesture. He headed down the street toward the two brothels. Two men had more to lose than all the rest of the town businessmen combined, and they were Jake Garwood and Adam Salter. As far as Longarm was concerned, one or the other—possibly even both—had hired the marksman who'd shot Georgia and then Elizabeth.

Of course, they'd vehemently deny the fact. But Longarm didn't much care about that. One way or another, he'd get a confession, even if it meant beating one or both men half to death.

Jake Garwood was standing in front of the more elegant of the two brothels, and when the owner of the Calico Cat saw Longarm marching up the street toward his business, he came forward.

"Marshal," he gushed, looking desperately afraid, "I know what you are thinking, but I didn't have anything to do with those shootings. I swear I didn't!"

"Where's Max?"

"He's still damn near unconscious from the beating and pistol-whipping you gave him earlier. There is no way he could have done the shootings."

"I'll decide that for myself. Take me to see him or I'll tear the doors off every crib you got!"

Garwood whirled around and led the way back to the Calico Cat. "He's in here," the owner said. "See for yourself."

Longarm slammed into the little room where Max lay on a bed. Under different circumstances, Longarm might almost have felt sorry for the bruiser because his face was a misshapen mass of purple flesh. The man's blackened lips were huge and swollen with blood and his jaw hung slack, displaying broken teeth. When Longarm went up beside his bed, Max couldn't even open his eyes.

"You really hurt him bad," Garwood said. "It's gonna take him months to recover, and I doubt he'll be half the man he was before."

"Did his brother come to visit?"

"No."

"Don't lie to me!"

"All right. All right. Otto *did* come."

"And what was his reaction?"

Garwood swallowed hard. "Listen, Otto works for Adam Salter. I take no responsibility for what he might have done."

Longarm wasn't listening. He was already heading across the street to the Speckled Bird brothel. Most likely, Otto was already on his way out of Oreville on the fastest horse he could find, but Longarm wasn't taking any chances. There was a score to settle and the law be damned!

Chapter 17

Longarm crashed into the Speckled Bird so hard that its slamming front door sounded like the boom of a cannon. He came to a halt in the middle of the parlor facing six of Adam Salter's girls.

"Where are they?" he growled.

"Otto is gone." The largest and brassiest-looking of the women stepped forward. One of her eyes was swollen completely shut and her lip was puffy. "He left here with a rifle and a big sack of money."

"What about Salter?"

"He's dead. Marshal, none of us knew what they were planning. But when we heard the shots and then the screams coming from where that meeting was being held, we figured it out."

"It was Otto that ambushed the Love Sisters tonight, wasn't it?"

"Yes. After the shots were fired, he burst in here looking wild and half-crazed. Then he ran into the back office, where he and Salter argued. We all heard Otto shouting about how he had to go on the run. He wanted money out of the safe, but Salter wouldn't give it to him, and so they fought."

"What happened?" Longarm asked.

"You can figure that one out," the woman snapped. "Otto beat Salter nearly senseless and made him open up the safe. Then Otto shot Salter three times. That's when I came rushing into the office and Otto decked me."

"You're lucky to still be alive."

"Did he kill one of the Love Sisters?" a whore asked, biting her lower lip.

"Yeah. Georgia O'Grady. She was the one they called Big Mamma."

"Oh, God," the girl breathed, covering her face. "That woman was here only yesterday telling us we needed to get out of this business. That maybe the Love Sisters could help."

"She's dead," Longarm told them as he started across the room toward Salter's office. "And there was another one shot. I don't know if she will live or not."

Adam Salter had been beaten savagely before he was shot three times in the head. The owner of the Speckled Bird lay in a pool of congealing blood. A large and expensive safe had been opened and its contents scattered. Otto had taken the money and left its door hanging open.

"What are we going to do now?" a blonde said, eyes dull with shock.

Longarm turned on the woman. "If I were you, I'd burn this hellhole to the ground and then I'd find another profession."

"I don't know how to do anything respectable."

"You can learn quick enough."

"There's no other place for women like us to go."

Longarm took a cigar from his coat pocket and lit it carefully. Then he dropped the burning match on some blood-spattered papers that littered the office floor. They caught fire almost instantly and flames leaped upward.

"Marshal! What . . ."

He pushed her out of the room. "It appears to me that

172

we have a fire. That means you and the others will *have* to do something else."

The young woman stared at him for a moment, and said, "I guess we might."

Longarm waited until the flames had really taken hold of the shabby rug and the bed where Adam Salter had "interviewed" so many of his girls. Then, he closed the door and headed for the street. As he passed the other women, he said, "If I were you, I'd grab whatever means most to you and get out of this building before it burns down on your heads."

"We will," the one with the eye swollen shut promised. "By the way, don't you want to know where Otto went?"

"I'll find him."

"It might help if you knew that he has friends that live about six miles north of Oreville. They are the only ones that would help him out, and even they'd turn on him if they knew he'd shot women tonight."

"What kind of a place is it?"

She spat blood on the floor. "I used to work there before I came here. It's this kind of a place and you'll see a red light hanging on the front porch."

"Thanks."

"Don't mention it. Just kill that sonofabitchin' Otto for all of us."

Longarm studied the faces of the six women. They were hard and pitiless. He doubted that any of them would go respectable, but that was not his worry. Smoke was already pouring into the dingy hallway. "You'd better get moving. That fire is heating up fast."

The woman spat blood again, and then she hurried off to empty her crib.

When Longarm rode out of town twenty minutes later, what he saw gave him a little cold comfort. The angry crowd and Garwood's own "soiled doves" had also set fire to the Calico Cat. The only one carrying a water bucket and attempting to douse the flames was Garwood himself. But one of his former girls tripped the man as he raced toward his burning building. Garwood hit the ground and skidded, bucket spilling water across the dirt. No one helped him up, but no one laughed, because there had been too much killing.

The rising wind was sending the flames and sparks high into the night sky. Longarm figured that the crowd had better start worrying about the entire town of Oreville catching fire and burning to the ground.

"Marshal!"

He twisted around in his saddle to see Peter Bradley come racing up the street. The man caught his breath and asked, "Was it Adam or Otto that shot those women?"

"Otto. He also killed and robbed Adam Salter."

Bradley stammered, "I want to come and help you catch that man."

"No," Longarm told him as the flames from both brothels leaped ever higher and smoke boiled into the ink-black sky. "I'd rather do this alone. Just . . . just take care of the girls and see that nothing else happens to them."

"I'll do it!"

Longarm reined his horse around and headed north. With any luck at all, he'd either kill or arrest Otto before midnight.

Before he'd ridden more than a couple of miles, it began to rain. The wind had been strengthening all afternoon, and the thunderstorm struck with a fury. Longarm had a warm coat but no rain slicker. His teeth were soon chattering so hard that he reined up in front of a little roadside saloon and went inside, thinking that he needed to get warm and dry. He was disappointed about the delay, but Otto wasn't going anyplace either in this foul weather.

Longarm thought there was a good chance it might even begin snowing before morning.

When he walked into the saloon, he saw that there were a half-dozen men at the bar. The interior was dim, and a cloud of blue smoke lay close to the ceiling. All the men at the bar turned and gave him a once-over, then turned back to their drinks and conversation.

"Rough night out there," the short, humpbacked bartender commented. "Not fit for man nor beast."

"No, it isn't," Longarm said. "Whiskey. Make it a double."

"You look near drowned," a young miner with restless eyes and an especially prominent nose told Longarm as he set his shot glass down and motioned for a refill.

"It's a bad one," Longarm said, coughing. "A fella could catch a dose of pneumonia out there on such a night."

"Where you headed?"

Longarm was purposefully vague when he said, "Just up the road."

"You goin' north . . . or south toward Oreville?"

"North."

"Me too. I got a job waiting at the Vulture Mine. You a miner?"

"Nope."

"Then what is your trade?"

Longarm didn't enjoy lying, but he'd found it healthier not to announce that he was a United States marshal unless he was about to act in an official capacity. So he hedged and replied, "I do this and that."

"This and that?" the miner repeated. "And you get paid?"

"Usually."

"Hey, fellas! This big jasper next to me says he does this 'n that!"

Longarm was relieved to see that no one seemed par-

175

ticularly interested in his employment status. When his double shot of whiskey arrived, he took a drink, and felt it burn all the way down to the bottom of his belly. He lit a cigar and headed over to an empty card table, hearing the crack of lightning and feeling the building shudder with every roll of thunder.

The miner followed him over to the table with his own drink. "Mind if I join you?"

Longarm didn't want conversation, but neither did he want to be unfriendly, so he gestured for the miner to have a seat.

"By the way, my name is Ernie. I sure wish I had a cigar to smoke."

"Have one of mine."

"Thank you kindly. I wish we were a few miles up the line and then we could stay at Rosie's Place."

"That would be a . . ."

"Whorehouse. It ain't as fancy as the Calico Cat or the Speckled Bird in Oreville, and there ain't but three girls work there, but they're a sight better company than we have in this saloon."

"I'm sure they are."

Ernie peered out the window. "I walked in here about an hour ago. Been waiting for the rain to let up so I could push on to Rosie's Place."

"Maybe it will."

"But maybe it won't," the man said. "You got a horse, don't you?"

"Yeah."

"We could ride it double up to Rosie's. I know them girls and I could save you a little money."

Longarm very much doubted that, but just nodded. "I'm fine right here."

"But the bartender will close this place up in a few hours. Then where will we go to get out of the rain?"

"I don't know."

"Rosie's Place is where we need to be," Ernie assured him. "Them three girls are probably all alone tonight on account of this storm. I think we could really get our money's worth with 'em on a cold, wet night like this. Maybe we could even spend *all* night with 'em!"

"Maybe."

"Look. Does your horse ride double?"

"I'm afraid not."

"Damn," the miner said. "I was afraid of that. Well, I walked all the way from Denver these past two months, and I can walk a few more miles tonight. With any luck, this rain will stop and we can go on to the Vulture Mine. You're a big, strong-lookin' fella like myself. Maybe they'd give a 'this'n that' like you a job."

"Not interested in becoming a miner."

"It pays good and the work is honest," Ernie assured him.

"I know," Longarm said, realizing the miner had taken his words as an insult on his profession. "But it's just not my line of work."

He signaled the bartender to bring him a bottle. When it arrived, he refilled his glass and also that of the young miner, who thanked him profusely. They drank for a few minutes in silence. Then Ernie tossed the last few drops of whiskey down and pushed himself to his feet. "Thanks again for the drink."

"Think nothing of it."

"Didn't catch your name."

"Custis."

"Well, Custis, I'm headin' for Rosie's Place."

"In this weather?"

"It's now or in a few hours, and I'd rather get the bad done so I can enjoy the good. Rosie's Place is open all night, and them brothers that run it will let you sleep on the floor or in their barn. They won't put you out in the rain like this bartender."

Longarm considered his words and took pity on the man. "Hold up. Maybe my horse will let you ride double after all."

"Why? He suddenly have a change of heart?" Ernie asked with a grin.

"Let's go."

Longarm ducked out into the rain and, if anything, the storm had intensified. Because he doubted that it would abate this night, he was determined to push on and have his showdown with Otto. He'd never been one to put off the hard or the dangerous, and he had no intention of starting that habit now.

The horse he'd rented in Oreville was a big, ugly bay gelding. Longarm checked his cinch and found it plenty tight. He mounted the bay, kicked his left foot out of his stirrup, and offered Ernie his hand.

The bay didn't buck when Ernie took his seat behind the saddle, and they rode north up the muddy road, heads down and feeling miserable.

"Won't be too much longer," Ernie shouted after what seemed like hours. "Rosie's Place is just up ahead a little ways."

Longarm thought that was wonderful news, even if it did bring him closer to danger.

"There it is! See the red light on the porch?"

Longarm saw it and reined the bay over to a hitching rail. He was chilled to the bone, and when Ernie slid off the rump of the bay, the miner went clear to his knees, telling Longarm that the man was as numb as himself.

"Come on in!"

"I see a barn over there and I'm going to put the horse up. I'll be right in," Longarm said, dismounting and leading the poor animal to shelter.

"Suit yourself, Custis! But I'd leave that plug out here and not give it a second thought. Horses can handle this weather better'n a man."

Longarm didn't pay Ernie any attention. He put his horse under shelter, unsaddled the wet, shivering beast, and even forked it some wet hay.

"That'll have to do you," he told the animal as he laid his saddle over a sawhorse and stuck his hands into his pockets in an attempt to thaw them out a little before he went inside to face Otto.

Ten minutes passed before he regained feeling in his fingers. In the meantime, the rain had worsened and the sky was filled with lightning.

Longarm hurried across the mud and when he reached the front door, he drew his gun and slipped it into his coat pocket. Stepping inside, he saw Ernie first, then two others, and one of them was Otto.

When Georgia's killer recognized Longarm, he dropped his glass of whiskey and made a stab for his gun. Longarm started to cry out to the fugitive that he was under arrest, but the words choked in his throat, so he waited an instant, then took quick aim and fired all in one fluid motion. His bullet caught Otto in the chest, slamming him back into the bar.

Ernie shouted something and dove for cover. Longarm watched the bald giant struggle to lift his six-gun, and when he managed to do that, Longarm shot him once more right between the eyes.

Then the third man in the room almost made a fatal miscalculation. His hand moved toward the gun on his hip, but when Longarm pivoted and took aim, the stranger threw up his hands and shouted, "Don't shoot!"

"Get your hands up higher!"

Longarm went over and disarmed the man. "Was Otto a real good friend?"

"Uh . . . no, sir!"

"I'm glad to hear that."

Two women peeked around a corner. They were both young, though neither would be considered pretty.

"Otto!" one of them cried, rushing to the dead man.

"He ambushed one woman tonight. Shot her dead in Oreville and wounded another," Longarm explained. "I'm a United States deputy marshal."

"My name is Zeke Smith," the stranger said. "And this is Claire and Pearl. Claire, Pearl, would you pour the marshal a drink?"

The girls jumped to do his bidding. Longarm didn't object. The rain pounded on the roof, but inside it was warm and dry. And maybe, if he had enough whiskey, one of the two girls would even begin to look pretty.

Chapter 18

When Longarm rode into Oreville the next afternoon, the sun was shining and the pines smelled fresh and sweet. The storm had passed, and although the roads were sloppy with mud, it hadn't snowed. The Speckled Bird and the Calico Cat were nothing more than mounds of charred rubble, some of which still steamed from last night's hard rain. Longarm knew without asking that Jake Garwood had been run out of town. The best news was that Elizabeth had not only survived his crude surgery, but was looking strong and obviously would recover.

"Miss Hanson agreed that she wouldn't be able to move for at least a month," Peter Bradley said. "And by then, I hope to have won her hand and heart."

"Good luck," Longarm offered, wondering if that Eastern girl could ever get used to living in Colorado. Denver perhaps, but he doubted she'd adapt to a mining town like Oreville.

His first order of business was the painful job of burying Georgia O'Grady. Longarm had a tough time getting past the funeral, but with the help of all the donations raised by the community, Georgia received a lavish send-off, and Longarm hoped her loving and generous spirit was at last reunited with her husband, Shamus.

With Elizabeth far too weak to travel, that left only Milly and Alice Fairchild, the granddaughter of the President. Longarm wasn't sure what they wanted to do, so after the funeral he said, "I'll return you safely to Denver. From there you can catch a train and go home."

"No," Alice told him without a moment's hesitation. "We've come to help the women of these mining towns and we mean to finish what we started."

"You want to remain in the Rockies?"

"That's right," Milly assured him. "And we've called another town meeting for tonight."

Longarm groaned inwardly because he feared for their lives. "Listen," he began, "you did all that you could, but—"

"If we quit now," Alice interrupted, "then Georgia O'Grady died in vain. We have to see this thing through, which means we must learn who needs our help and then make sure that their names are on our list to receive money."

"Alice, has it occurred to you that after the shootings, no one might dare to step forward?"

"We'll find out tonight." Alice handed him a new flyer. It wasn't much different from the first one, and Longarm read it at a glance. "Ladies," he began, "I—"

"We're not giving up on the Love Sisters," Milly warned him in a tone that brooked no interference. "We say that realizing some other gunman could be out there waiting to ambush us like he did Georgia and Elizabeth, but this is something that we must finish."

Longarm walked away shaking his head.

That night in Oreville was one that he would never forget. In contrast to the first deadly town meeting, this one was quiet and purposeful. Almost every one of the ladies who'd worked at the Speckled Bird and the Calico Cat came dressed in their most respectable outfits. They behaved like ladies. While Milly, Alice, and finally the young widow Helen Clum gave inspirational and emotional speeches about how things should and would improve for all mining women, the former soiled doves cried and applauded with great enthusiasm. Perhaps even more amazing was that the hundred or so miners who stood a respectable distance from the gathering cheered and clapped their hands for each of the Love Sisters.

"I want to marry you, Helen!" a tall, clean-cut young man shouted at the top of his lungs. "And I want to be a *real* father to Ted and John!"

"Oh, I accept!" the widow cried, running toward the caller. When the pair embraced, the crowd roared with approval.

Longarm didn't wait around to hear more speech-making. He entered a saloon and limped up to the bar. The lonely bartender smiled. "Everyone is outside listening, so it's just you and me for the moment, Marshal. What is your pleasure?"

"Whiskey. A bottle of your best."

"Anything you say."

When the bottle came, Longarm poured a tumbler full, then paused for a moment before announcing, "I want to make a toast and that takes two. Fill a glass on me."

The bartender produced an oversized glass and slapped it down so that it could be filled. "Who are we toasting?"

"Mrs. Georgia O'Grady."

The bartender's brow wrinkled. "I'm sorry, but who is she?"

"You might know her as . . . Big Mamma," Longarm solemnly answered.

The bartender's questioning glance was replaced by

a sad smile. "Ah, yes! Now there was one hell of a woman!"

Longarm agreed, and as he drank the good whiskey and remembered that big, beautiful woman, he turned his back to the bar and quietly wiped away a tear.

Watch for

**LONGARM AND THE MAD BOMBER'S
BRIDE**

265th novel in the exciting LONGARM series
from Jove

Coming in December!

T